Also by M

Bobby's Boy (Lanarkshire Strays)

Naebody's Hero (Lanarkshire Strays)

Head Boy (Lanarkshire Strays)

Paddy's Daddy

The Man Who Sold His Son (Lanarkshire Strays)

Lanarkshire Strays: Collected Edition

dEaDINBURGH: Alliances (Din Eidyn Corpus 2)

dEaDINBURGH: Origins (Din Eidyn Corpus 3)

dEaDINBURGH: Collected Edition

These titles are available on kindle and paperback from Amazon, US and UK as well as other formats at Paddy's Daddy Publishing.

Copyright

This book is a work of fiction. Names, characters, places and incidents are either the product of the author's imagination or are used fictitiously. Any resemblance to real persons, alive or dead, is coincidental and not intended by the author.

Second Edition, 2015

Text Copyright©2015 Mark Wilson

All rights reserved.

ISBN-13: 978-1507866597

ISBN-10: 1507866593

No part of this book may be reproduced, or stored in a retrieval system, or transmitted in any form or by any means, electronic, mechanical, photocopying, recording, or otherwise, without express permission of Mark Wilson and Paddy's Daddy Publishing.

Published by Paddy's Daddy Publishing.

www.facebook.com/markwilsonbooks

www.markwilsonbooks.com

Follow on Twitter: @bellshillwilson

Cover image by Paul McGuigan Photography

Dedication

For Michelle Wilson

Writing this book I drew on a lot of influences, but none more so than that of all the strong women in my life, past and present.

Rena Wilson, Natalie Wilson, Michelle Wilson, Cara Wilson.

All a small part of Alys Shephard and a huge part of my heart.

"Though she be but little, she is fierce." – William Shakespeare.

Acknowledgements

I'd like to thank the following people for their support in writing this novel:

Thanks to my regular test-readers Derek Graham, Gayle Karabelen. Derek suggested linking the plague to the Ring of Roses rhyme. Thanks for that, dude. Gayle always agrees to read for me without hesitation.

Very Special thanks to Jayne Doherty for her continued support of my writing career. Always ready to help, your support is much appreciated and never taken for granted. Jayne is ever-reliable and always ready to give an honest opinion. Thank you so much.

Special thanks also to fellow writers Keith Nixon and Ryan Bracha. Both have been a tremendous support and source of inspiration and always make themselves available for advice or to just talk nonsense about whatever. Reading their books pushes me to be a better writer. Thanks also to Bracha for letting me have his name.

Thanks also to Paul McGuigan of PMCG Photography for lending me his talents shooting key locations from the book around Edinburgh on a very dreech afternoon.

A huge thank you, as always to my wife Natalie Wilson for unwavering encouragement and support. Twenty years with me isn't an easy task.

dEaDINBURGH

VANTAGE

by

MARK WILSON

Paddy's Daddy Publishing

Prologue

Edinburgh, Scotland

2051

Joey regained consciousness, becoming slowly aware that he still lay on the grass, beneath her. *She hadn't left him*. Whirling, jabbing her Sai, leaping and kicking, she was a lethal whirlwind of blows and strikes and death. Centimetres from his prone body she did what had to be done. That's what she always did. He rolled over from his back onto his side, curled his body inward and ripped off his right boot. One glance at the red stain blossoming out across the fabric of his sock from the big toe of his foot told him that it was all over. The nail had been bitten through. He watched the blood spread, detachedly noting to himself how like a poppy it looked with his toe at the centre of the blood flower. *Why is she still here?*

Glancing across at his left hand, he noticed that an injury he'd taken there was bleeding freely also.

Trying to stand, he braced himself with the palm of his right hand pressed into the mud and blood, but found that his legs weren't listening and crumpled back to the ground. He tried twice more to stand before she kneed him in the shoulder, knocking him back to a curled position. She'd fought harder still and made a three-second gap in the fight to turn her attention to him. Three seconds was three times as long as she'd need, but that's how she was: well prepared. He'd taught her that. They'd taught each other so much in the too-little time they'd spent together.

Instead of the terror he'd expected, a peaceful acceptance slid over him. He didn't raise his hands to protect himself and he didn't close his eyes. Placing one foot either side of him in a strike position, she raised her third Sai, the deadliest, swirled it around in her palm to a stabbing position and threw herself at him. As she struck, he did close his eyes. Not for himself, not to welcome the black darkness he still missed from Mary King's Close, but for *her*. She shouldn't have to look in his eyes as she killed him. Silenced him.

Thank you, Alys, Joey's voice whispered inside his head. Outside, Joseph MacLeod was still.

Edinburgh
Scotland
2047

dEaDINBURGH: Vantage • 4

Chapter 1

Joey

Eyes still closed, he rose from his concrete bunk, sitting and rotating his hips to swing his legs out and over the edge of the sleeping space. Feeling the concrete crunch beneath his booted feet, Joey stood and took the three steps to his right before reaching out to pick up the box that lay on a shelf fixed to the ancient walls. Despite the darkness, he was unhurried and his hands found the box of wax crayons first time. With his other hand Joey flicked open the box and ran the tip of his index finger along the uniformly arranged crayons, searching for one that was a little shorter than the others. Finding his crayon, he tossed the box back into the darkness, hearing it thump onto the shelf as he fished his disposable cigarette lighter from the pocket of his denims.

Although he hadn't opened his eyes since waking, Joey clenched them a little more tightly in anticipation of the coming light. Sparking his lighter, he turned his face away from the glare that hurt his eyes, even filtered red through his eyelids. Bringing his hands together, Joey lit the end of a crayon and slowly peeked open his eyes, allowing them to adjust to the light. He smiled wryly to himself as he registered that the little, bright flame's colour didn't match the candle's purple colour. Despite having lit hundreds of crayon-candles to break the darkness over the years, part of him still hoped each time for something other than the uninteresting, standard orange flame.

Holding the crayon-candle out from his body, he reached behind a dresser, touching the edge of his bow which he'd concealed there. On confirming the safety of his only belonging, Joey left the crypt his *family* occupied and made his way through the black alleys towards the main chambers where Communion would be taking place later that day. Watching the glow from his makeshift candle dance cheerfully along the walls as he walked, he smiled to himself, satisfied. He had a few chores to do and the Children of Elisha to feed, but if he worked quickly he hoped to have enough time to take a trip up to the surface and along to the castle's esplanade to practice before Communion began.

It'd been three months since the last Communion; three months since he'd heard a voice that didn't vibrate with dryness, dust and hunger. The voice of someone alive. The only sounds he'd heard in those weeks had been scraping of boot on stone, of the residents walking through the darkness of Mary King's Close, the underground town they lived in; those and the groans of the dead as they pressed against the fences and roamed the cobbles above.

The Brotherhood, who'd taken him in as an infant, had taken vows of silence and of servitude to the risen dead, whom they called the Children of Elisha. Believing that the meek had finally inherited the earth, The Brotherhood believed that the Children of Elisha were God's chosen and that The Brotherhood were spared solely to serve them.

As lonely as Joey felt sometimes in the darkness of The Brotherhood's crypts, it was the only life he'd ever known. Despite not wholly subscribing to their dogma, he partook in their ceremonies and traditions out of respect and gratitude. Mostly he took part out of boredom. As a fifteen-year-old, he was given a little leeway with the traditions and allowed to wander around above ground, but this was expected to change when he was eighteen and took his final vows of servitude.

Rounding the next corner, Joey noted that some light was visible now in the tunnel system. This meant that the torch-lighters were doing their work in preparation for the Communion ceremony. Communion week was the only time the residents bothered to light the torches, preferring the gentle light of a candle, or a crayon, to find their way around the maze of underground streets.

"Elisha's blessings on you, Young Brother." The man, a torch-lighter, made a circle with his right hand in the centre of his chest as he spoke.

Joey returned the gesture which The Brotherhood used to symbolise the infinite life of the Children of Elisha.

"And also upon you."

Despite not liking the torch-lighter much, he had to admit that it was good to hear a living voice again.

"We'll see you at Communion, Brother Joseph?" It was more an accusation than a question.

"Wouldn't miss it." Joey supressed a grin.

At one time he and the torch-lighter, a nineteen-year-old named Bobby, had run together through the underground crypts and the cobbled streets of the Royal Mile above, ignoring the disapproving glares of the elder Brothers. Now that Bobby was a fully-inducted member of The Brotherhood he didn't have time for fun. Bobby was too busy honouring and feeding the dead and punishing himself for being alive, along with the rest of them.

Joey couldn't imagine never going to the surface again; never seeing the sun or the moon or feeling the fresh Edinburgh air cut into his face. His adoptive father expected – no, that wasn't right – hoped that he would settle down, as Bobby had, when his time came. As grateful as he was for being given a home by The Brotherhood, Joey had no intention of confining his world to the dank crypts. His refusal, when it came, would most likely mean that he had to leave Mary King's Close and everything he'd ever known, but he reckoned that it was better to be alone on the surface with the dead than in silence and servitude with those below.

With a final scowl, Bobby turned his back on him and reached up to touch the flaming torch in his hand to the freshly prepared one on the wall. Joey resisted the urge to kick his ladder and moved past him.

"Have fun, Bobby," he offered as he left.

Continuing along to the main chamber, Joey mechanically completed the chores he'd been assigned: clean the altar, fill the bowls, and decant the Carrionite into the wooden bowl. By the time he'd completed his tasks, he reckoned that he had enough time before the ceremony to take a trip up to the Castle esplanade with his bow for some practice.

Most of the tunnels and crypts on the route back to his cell were now lit and glowing orange. Despite the number of flames blazing throughout the underground town, little in the way of heat was added to the environment. It didn't seem to matter how many fires were lit or clothes worn. Down here, the cold rock absorbed every ounce of heat and a person's bones remained chilled. It was a miserable place to exist but the thought of his imminent trip to the surface lifted Joey's spirits.

Joey suddenly became aware of someone nearby, in the tunnels up ahead. A scrape of leather on stone, *that whistle*. The figure, clad in leathers, boots and gloves with his ever-present satchel over his shoulder, blades in sheaths on this thighs and the white rectangle of his vicar's collar peeking out from the neck of his black shirt, stood passively staring at Joey.

Padre Jock.

Reputedly a minister before the dead rose, Jock was afforded a respect and position that no one else in Mary King's Close came close to. Although not a member of The Brotherhood, Jock had lived there in the crypts with them for as long as Joey could remember. Aside from himself and a few of the younger, more insolent kids, Jock was the only other person who would regularly venture up to the surface. Joey would've liked that about the old padre, if only he didn't give him the creeps.

Often when on the surface, and occasionally here in the crypts, Joey would hear or sense Padre Jock watching him from the end of a tunnel or a street. Whenever Joey looked up or waved at Jock, the padre would disappear round a corner only to reappear later, watching passively until he was seen again.

Padre Jock had watched him so often that Joey had started to feel a little odd when the cleric wasn't a few streets behind or ahead of him. The man never said a word to him. Whenever Joey had tried to talk to him, or shouted at him to get lost, Jock simply threw the boy a disdainful glare and disappeared.

Nervous as he was, Joey was in a hurry and didn't have time for the old man's nonsense.

"Is there something you want, Padre?"

Jock threw him the same scowl he always did and turned to depart. Joey felt his anger rise and decided to provoke him.

"Gies a wee look at of your Bible," he shouted at Jock's back.

Instantly Jock whipped around and covered the short distance between them. Bringing his face level with Joey's he scratched a finger along the top of his satchel, filling the tunnel with a screech of nail on leather. "You of all people do not want to read my... *Bible,*" Jock whispered calmly.

Up close, Joey gained a new appreciation for Padre Jock. The man was huge, at least six-four. Joey swallowed a lump from his throat, lowered his eyes to look at the satchel, and then lifted them back to Jock's face. He was scared but he was more angry than frightened and forced his voice to remain steady. "Everyone says you used that Bible in there to beat a group of the dead into silence. I want to see it."

It was true. Everyone did say that Jock had killed a church full of the Children of Elisha, his former flock, by bashing their brains in with his Bible on the day the plague hit, but no one had ever asked him to verify the story. No one spoke to Jock at all.

The two of them stared at each other for several very long seconds until Jock broke the moment by releasing a loud, mocking laugh that echoed along the crypt's walls, startling Bobby further along the tunnel.

"Ha! It's about time." Jock smiled a smile that to Joey was more disturbing than his scowl and melted back into the darkness.

Joey released a long breath he hadn't realised he'd been holding, shook his head and started back towards his crypt to retrieve his bow. If he hurried there would be enough time before Communion to practice with it.

Chapter 2

Alys

STANDING FROM A CROUCH Alys leaned back, stretching her vertebrae to their maximum extension. She gave a few sharp turns to her left and her right, loosening off her hips. Finally Alys leaned forward and down, wrapping her arms around the backs of her legs, bringing her forehead to her shins.

Jennifer sighed. "Every time, Alys? You won't always have time for that nonsense, you know."

Alys was sick of her mother's sharpness and performed the routine simply to provoke her. She was the most accomplished fighter in her age group, and better than the classes senior to hers also, but nothing ever seemed good enough.

"Just limbering up," she said flatly.

Her mother pursed her lips.

"Does an animal limber up? Do the dead limber up?"

Alys ignored her and took her ready stance. Jennifer sighed and assumed her own ready position. Stepping forward, Alys delivered a series of sharp blows with her hands, alternating between her mother's face and chest. Jennifer blocked each of them easily, but she was supposed to. Alys had used the flurry as a cover for the kick she shot out at Jennifer's knee. This too failed to connect as the older woman slipped her front foot back ten centimetres, causing Alys' kick to jab into the ground. Jennifer stepped onto her daughter's front foot, trapping it and preventing her daughter stepping away from the vicious hammer punch she flashed out with lightning speed.

Standing over her prone daughter, Jennifer checked her watch.

"Five seconds this time, Alys. You're getting better."

Alys glared up her for a second before picking herself up out of the mud. She spat a mouthful of blood onto the ground a few centimetres from her mother's feet.

"Again," she demanded.

Jennifer smiled her approval and moved in to deliver another lightning blow to her daughter's face.

An hour later Alys stood in the centre of the practice plot. Dripping with sweat and with the smell of her own blood in her nostrils, she glared at Jennifer who stood calm and impassive; just as she'd been when their practice had begun.

"Again," Alys growled.

Jennifer approved but no shred of that approval showed on her face.

"No," she said simply and walked away. As she left, she briefly turned back to face her daughter.

"Remember to take the offering up to The Brotherhood's gates."

Alys didn't reply, choosing instead to stand in the rain and let it cool her anger as it washed away the sweat and blood she'd shed. The rain and cold of an Edinburgh autumn was as familiar to her as the sunshine and relative warmth of its springtime. Her life had been lived, exposed; farming, fighting and living under canvas, here in the beauty of Princes Street Gardens. Most of her community believed that they were free. Free to farm and eat and train and live under the Edinburgh sky in the shade of the craggy castle. Alys just felt trapped.

The only way she could leave the Gardens permanently was to convince her mother that she was ready to become a Ranger. That she could fight. Still standing in a ready stance, fists quivering and face up towards the falling rain, Alys finally relaxed her bunched-up muscles. Standing simply with her weary arms at her sides, something glinted and caught her eye. She looked up towards the Castle's Esplanade, noting that *he* was there again. She'd never once been allowed to venture outside her community's fences. The farthest she'd walked was to deliver the Garden's offerings up to The Brotherhood's gates on the Royal Mile.

Alys couldn't understand why her people continued to feed the reclusive Brotherhood and had grown to resent them. She'd been taught to fight, to earn her place in the community, and to fight to keep it. Her community didn't allow men inside its gates, believing that their weakness was a risk. So why were they helping feed a group of men who were too deluded to grow or scavenge their own food? Yes, she resented them, but most of all she resented the boy with the bow.

The first time she'd seen the boy had been on a food run up to The Brotherhood's gates on Bank Street around five years ago. She'd been ten years old and had dutifully carried the container of fresh foods to the gates, traipsing sullenly alongside her mother. After Jennifer had placed the food at the fence line, she'd turned and begun making the short journey back to Princes Street Gardens. Out of curiosity, Alys stayed.

She'd never seen a member of The Brotherhood. She'd heard plenty of stories – of how they lived in their crypts, how they worshipped the dead, wandered among the dead creatures and even fed them their own blood – but hadn't see one of the men in person. It wasn't just their strange lifestyle that drew her; she hadn't seen a male since her father had *gone*. She'd asked her mother many times in the early weeks following his departure, and several times in the intervening ten years or so, but always received the same gruff reply from Jennifer.

"He's just gone, Alys."

So she'd waited, around the corner, peeking at the fences from behind the edge of a building. After a few hours a boy had appeared. He was dressed in simple, slim-legged black denims, a long-sleeved black T with his thumbs poking through holes at the ends of the sleeves and a trash bag with holes cut for his arms to slip through. Over his head a hood concealed most of his face, but a few locks of very blond hair strayed out from underneath. Warily he'd come close to the fence, opened the gate and retrieved the offering. As quickly as he'd come, he left again.

Alys couldn't say why but she waited in that same spot a little longer until eventually the same boy appeared once more. He stood at the fence, staring at her. This time, he didn't look nervous.

"Hello? Are you still there?"

Alys' eyes opened wide at his greeting. She'd been taught that The Brotherhood wouldn't or couldn't speak. Guardedly she came out from her spot and approached the fence.

"All right?" the boy had asked, with an awkward smile.

Alys simply nodded, narrowing her eyes as she noted the quiver on his back and the bow in his left hand. Realising that she felt threatened, the boy placed his bow on the ground, stood straight and pulled down his hood to reveal a head full of shaggy blond hair and beautifully vibrant green eyes. He was around the same age as she was. That in itself was strange, she'd thought that The Brotherhood were all grown men. That he stood smiling at her with excitement in his eyes and a grin on his face took her completely by surprise. She'd heard that as well as being silent, The Brotherhood were perpetually numbed by a substance they inhaled to commune with the dead. This boy was anything but numb. His eyes danced with excitement. He had cocked his head to the side and was assessing her as she assessed him.

Approaching him, Alys asked, "What do you want?"

"To say thank you." He nodded back towards where his people lived. "For the kindness."

"If I had any choice I wouldn't bring it," she blurted out. "Your people don't deserve it."

The boy's eyes lost a little of their sparkle and his smile flattened. Clearly hurt, he picked up his bow, raised his hood once more and turned to head towards the Castle. After walking a few feet, he turned to face her again.

"Well, thanks anyway."

With that he took off at a run, executing a few little leaps and somersaults using the masonry and steps of the local buildings as launch pads. Alys heard him laugh as he whirled and ran his way up to the Castle Esplanade.

She'd seen him many times since then; practicing with his bow, leaping and somersaulting through the Royal Mile and along the Castle buildings. She hated him for how carefree, how happy he seemed. He trained hard, and that impressed her. He practiced with his bow every day, but why should he be so free, so happy, when her people, when she, had to work so hard to provide for him and his people?

She imagined him laughing with his Brothers at how gullible her community was for providing them with supplies. As time went on, she'd learned that the rest of The Brotherhood were indeed as silent, as disconnected from the world, as her people had described them as being.

This boy – the boy with the bow – was the exception. She hated him even more for his ability to free himself of the constraints of his community and trained all the harder, fuelled by contempt for him, by jealousy, and in the hopes that she may one day discover a way to be as free as he seemed.

Alys lowered her head and looked at her trembling hands. She'd made contact with her mother twice during their session. It was twice more than she'd ever managed before, and whilst her blows hadn't really had any impact, the mere fact that she'd landed them lifted her spirits. She was definitely getting better. Placing her arms around herself in a hug, Alys took a last look up at the Castle to see the boy with the bow pulling another arrow from his quiver, lining up his shot and releasing yet another perfect arrow. The satisfaction she'd felt at her progress disappeared and she took off on a run up the Playfair Steps. *The Brotherhood can wait for their free meal. I've got stamina to build.*

Alys punished her legs running up and walking down the long staircase for the next sixty minutes. Hunched over on all fours at the top, she looked along the mound and up to the Castle. Another convulsion racked her; she threw up what bile she had left in her stomach and glared upwards, daring the boy with the bow to show his face.

Satisfied that she had nothing left, no reserve of energy with which to pull herself up the stairs once more, she made her way down the gentle swooping slope of The Mound, returning to Princes Street

Gardens and the task of preparing The Brotherhood's offering.

Padre Jock's Journal

In 1645 the bubonic plague (or the Black Death) raged through the populace. Millions had died worldwide and the city's residents were beginning to feel the effects of the disease. In a desperate attempt to isolate the infected and to save the remaining residents, the council leaders forced the sick into the underground streets of Mary King's Close and sealed them in. Beneath the cobbles of old Edinburgh the infected, who begged to be released, suffered and were ignored. Eventually forgotten, they were abandoned and left roaming the underground streets of the crypts below.

Above, on the surface, the children danced on Edinburgh's cobbles, joyful that the plague had been contained. According to legend they sang,

Ring-a-ring-a-roses,

A pocket full of posies;

Atishoo! Atishoo!

We all fall down.

A rosy rash, they alleged, was a symptom of the plague, and posies of herbs were carried as protection and to ward off the smell of the disease. Sneezing or coughing was a final fatal symptom and *all fall down* was exactly what happened. The people of Mary King's Close were abandoned mercilessly.

As all bacteria do, the plague bacteria evolved and it mutated.

Underground for hundreds of years, and some survivors had children, they became something other than human: undead, shuffling through the dark crypts racked by a 400-year hunger, a ring-a-roses rash emblazoned on their left cheeks marking them as infected.

On New Year's Day 2015, the city leaders re-opened The Close, with the intention of erecting a memorial to the ancient plague victims and using the newly-opened Close for tourism. The Close's residents poured out from their tomb and spread a new plague through the city. One that killed and hijacked what remained of its host and was characterised by the rash, that and the fact that the host was dead but somehow walking around with a hunger for human flesh.

The word Zombie was thrown around in those first few days, but no one could say it without smiling. Zombies were make-believe, something from the movies or TV. These creatures in our city were real. We took to calling them The Ringed because of the characteristic rash. Some people still called them Zoms.

The Ringed spilled out into an Edinburgh full of partygoers and New Year celebrants. The plague spread quickly. The Ringed began appearing everywhere.

Within a day, many of Edinburgh's residents were infected. Within a week, the UK government, recruiting the armed forces, had erected a huge and extensive fence around the circumference of the city bypass, quarantining the city. Edinburgh was declared an official no man's land. A dead zone, its residents left for dead and to the dead.

I had a chance to leave before they sealed us in, but stayed to help the survivors. I never thought for a second that they, the world outside, would leave us here and forget about us. For that first decade of isolation, I always believed that, sooner or later, they'd find a cure, that they would release us. I should have remembered my history.

Chapter 3

Joey

Clattering his disassembled bow and the quiver into their hiding place, Joey retrieved his Communion robe, a black woollen poncho, from his dresser and took off at a sprint towards the main chamber where the ceremony was seconds from beginning. Brother Andrew, his guardian, wouldn't be amused at his tardiness but it was too late to worry about that now.

Time had slipped away from him, as it always did, while he'd smoothly loaded and released arrow after arrow from his bow up on the Castle Esplanade. Standing perfectly still in the cold Edinburgh wind, he'd focused on the centre of his makeshift targets and released a series of perfect shots, one after the other. With each arrow lipping smoothly from his bow, Joey felt more relaxed, more alive. During his practice session he'd become aware that someone watched him. Assuming that Padre Jock was tailing him again, he ignored the presence. He raised his left arm and primed the bow for another shot when a flash of movement from the Gardens below caught his attention. Lowering the bow, Joey narrowed his eyes and focused on the black-haired figure standing alone, face up to the rainy sky. It was *her*.

Joey didn't like her. They'd only met a handful of times over the years, but each time they had the girl had stared daggers at him. She seemed truly furious whenever they met. Joey wondered how someone who lived out in the open, under the sky and in such beautiful surroundings, someone so free, someone so... beautiful, could be so miserable.

Watching her march back towards the community's main tent, Joey sighed, raised his bow and refocused on his shot. As he pulled the string back to his nose, pulling tension into the string of his takedown recurve bow, he said a silent thank you to whoever had left the bow for him in his chamber on the morning of his tenth birthday. At times his bow was the only thing that gave him any joy.

In the five years he'd owned it, Joey had stopped wondering who had left it there for him; it was pointless. No one in The Brotherhood owned anything. Aside from some ragged clothes, each of them had discarded any personal items when they'd taken their vows. That left only Padre Jock, and there was simply no way that the creepy minister had given him such a gift.

Brother Andrew knew he had the bow and, naturally, disapproved, but had allowed him to keep it and to practice with it on the surface, on two conditions: that he didn't allow any of the other young Brothers to use it and that he handed it over for disposal upon taking his vows. That wasn't going to happen.

Five years spent perfecting his technique had made the bow part of his arm. Joey figured that he'd cross that particular bridge when he came to it.

Approaching the main chamber, Joey halted his sprint, smoothed down his robe and painted on a convincing look of serenity. He pretended not to notice Brother Andrew scowling angrily at him as he took his place on a bench towards the rear of the chamber. As he sat, a loud creak of protest from the wooden bench echoed around the chamber. Father Grayson, The Brotherhood's patriarch, stopped mid-sentence and glowered at him for a moment. Joey picked a spot on the concrete floor and stared at it until the chamber filled once again with Father Grayson's commanding voice.

"We," he boomed, "Elisha's chosen, have performed our sacred duties through four decades. It has fallen to us to walk with and care for the Children of Elisha who have inherited the world, by God's will."

"BY GOD'S WILL," a hundred strained throats cried back, sore and unused for three months. The Brotherhood winced collectively as they broke the silence. Some held their ears.

Grayson continued. "Today, we give the daily offering of our blood so that the Children of Elisha may continue in their sacred existence. "

"BLESSINGS BE UPON THE CHILDREN," the Brothers croaked.

Grayson spread out his arms in a crucifixion pose, a gesture made to include everyone in the chamber. His long black robes billowed slightly.

"Today we receive our Communion directly with Elisha and his Children."

"BLESSINGS UPON THE HOLY ELISHA." A ripple of excitement and of anticipation moved through the chamber as Grayson reached for the simple wooden bowls containing the Carrionite.

"Step forward, Brothers, and commune with our blessed Saint and his Children," Grayson commanded.

Joey still had his head bowed but glanced up occasionally to watch the procession of Brothers in single file take Communion one at a time. As Brother

Andrew approached the altar, Grayson scooped out a portion of the powdered Carrionite from the bowl with a silver teaspoon, tipped the powder onto the altar, drew a line around ten centimetres long and watched with approval as Brother Andrew filled his nose, inhaling every speck of the Communion powder.

"Blessed are we," said Grayson

"Blessed we are," Andrew replied, drawing the ceremonial blade in his right hand across the palm of his left. He clenched his fist over a large goblet, allowing a stream of his blood to flow into it. Finally he wrapped a clean cotton cloth around the wound and made way for the next Brother.

As Andrew walked slowly back to his bench, Joey noted the familiar glaze had already slid over Brother Andrew's eyes. His facial muscles had relaxed and he was effectively dragging his dulled limbs back to sit in his allotted position on bench two. The Carrionite kicked in fully as he sat, making his gaze and countenance look so much like that of the Children of Elisha that Joey might have considered running from the chamber, if he hadn't seen the effect on the face of his Brothers dozens of times before. As he continued to observe Andrew, he saw him slip into the comatose state, characteristic of the Carrionite.

"Joseph MacLeod, come forward," Grayson boomed.

Joey shot up to a standing position, in shock at having been called by name. Kids Joey's age didn't take communion; only fully initiated Brothers did so. He must've screwed something up when preparing the Carrionite. Public humiliation followed by atonement was very much a favoured technique in Father Grayson's repertoire.

Joey ignored the murmurs of those who hadn't taken Communion yet and pushed past the catatonic bodies and floppy limbs of those who had until he reached the altar. Looking up at Grayson, he asked, "How may I serve you, Father?"

Grayson didn't answer, but lifted his spoon into the Carrionite and spread out an offering for Joey.

He shook his head at the patriarch.

"Father, I'm not of age."

Grayson didn't reply, but used an open-palm gesture to indicate that Joey should take Communion. *Was it a test? Was he being punished? Would he be wrong to take the Carrionite, or wrong to refuse?*

Hearing someone enter the quiet chamber, Joey glanced quickly over his shoulder towards the door to see Padre Jock strut in. It wasn't unusual to see the old man at these events. He never took part but rather seemed to find some amusement in the ritual and pomp of Communion. Jock looked straight at Joey, then at the Carrionite in front of him, and finally threw Joey a look of pure contempt before leaving.

dEaDINBURGH: Vantage • 33

The look cut Joey to the bone. *Who the hell is he to judge me?*

Father Grayson reached down and placed a hand gently on Joey's shoulder. "Take it," he whispered.

"Why?" Joey asked.

Grayson's eyebrows rose in surprise but he held his anger and spoke softly.

"Some Brothers, for their own safety and for that of his Brothers, must be initiated early. Take it."

Releasing the boy's shoulder, Grayson rose to his full height, spread his arms wide and yelled, "Today Brother Joseph leaves his old life, his childhood behind. Even one such as he," Grayson pointed a long finger at Joey, "even this boy, despite his rebellious nature, despite the nature of his arrival into our midst, even he is welcomed into our sacred Brotherhood."

Joey's ears pricked up at this. He'd almost never heard anyone refer to the fact that he wasn't born into The Brotherhood, almost never heard any of the Brothers refer to how he came to Mary King's Close as a baby. Exasperated at the futility, he'd stopped asking Brother Andrew years ago. That Grayson was mentioning his arrival in a public forum like this was astonishing. *Was he about to tell him who his parents were?*

"Full members of The Brotherhood are privy to all of our secrets, young Joseph."

Grayson indicated again for him to take the Carrionite. Looking out at the assembled Brothers, Joey searched their faces for help. Bobby, Andrew, former friends all either turned their gaze away from his desperate eyes or were too high on Carrionite to notice. Joey found himself wishing that Padre Jock would come back to scowl at him, to inject some will into him with the anger he projected towards everyone in his line of sight. But Jock was gone, as disgusted with his participation in Communion as the Brothers would be with his non-participation.

Grayson had trapped him. He'd made no secret that he felt Joey didn't belong in Mary King's Close. He didn't like outsiders, people *not born to the service*. Joey had no idea why The Brotherhood had ever taken him in as a baby. It damn sure wasn't out of compassion as The Brotherhood would dutifully leave any living person to be 'blessed', to be fed on by the Children of Elisha. If he refused the Carrionite, Grayson would make him leave. If he partook, he'd be just like *them*.

"Do it," Grayson screeched at him, losing his composure in his eagerness.

Looking around the chamber, filled with the passive faces and bodies of the only people he'd ever known, Joey made his decision.

"No," he said simply and left for his chambers.

Sprinting at full-speed along the tunnels of The Close, Joey reached his chamber within seconds and began pulling together all of his belongings. He had maybe twenty minutes before The Brotherhood began to rouse from their Communion and came for him. Grayson wouldn't tolerate a non-believer in the underground town and would more than likely make him an offering to the Children of Elisha.

Pulling his clothes and possessions into the middle of the cold, damp chamber he'd called home for fifteen years, Joey packed what spare clothes he had into a rough canvas rucksack along with some other items, including a pouch of Carrionite. He dressed quickly in black denims, thermal long-sleeved T and sturdy hiking boots, all scavenged from a mountaineering shop.

Assembling his bow, Joey slipped his quiver full of arrows over his shoulder and onto his back and darted through the chamber archway, running straight into Padre Jock's rock-hard chest. Thrown onto his ass, he launched himself back up onto his feet.

"Get the hell out of my way," he ordered the old minister.

Silently, Jock stood aside and offered his palm out towards the door allowing Joey to dart through.

"Good for you, son." Jock smiled to himself as he listened to Joey's footsteps race through the tunnel.

Performing a quick check on his knives and other equipment, Padre Jock strolled off towards the main chamber at a leisurely pace.

Chapter 4

Alys

"Go to sleep, Stephanie," Alys whispered to her younger cousin who was sitting up in bed.

"I can't. Can I come with you, Alys?"

She was a sweet kid. Ten years old and at that age when she was just beginning to become a competent fighter, under the tuition of the council, but was still young enough to consider her combat training fun.

Alys smiled down at her in her bed and pulled on her leather jacket. Tucking her three Sai into their places – one on each thigh, one on her belt – she told Steph once again, "No, maybe next time, but not tonight."

Alys tucked the girl back into bed and slipped out through the gap in her canvas tent. Once outside she looked up at the crescent moon, pulled her collar up against the breeze and took off at a slow run towards the gates of The Brotherhood.

Unable to get the boy with the bow out of her thoughts, Alys had decided earlier in the evening to visit the Castle Esplanade and spend some time training there, where *he* trained. She deserved the freedom; she'd earned it. Unfortunately her mother disagreed and still demanded that she did not leave the safety of their fenced community until *she* deemed her ready. Alys was supremely confident in her abilities to defend herself and dispatch any threat, of either the living or the dead variety. Besides, the Esplanade was Brotherhood territory and they rarely ventured outside of their underground town, certainly never after dark. Aside from the boy with the bow. Something shifted in her gut once more at the thought of him and the freedom he had but didn't deserve. *I deserve it*, she told herself.

In order to reach the Esplanade, Alys would have to go through The Brotherhood gates and walk along through the Royal Mile, up Castlehill and onto the Castle grounds. She didn't know that part of the city, but from the layout she was able to see from The Gardens below, it looked like a straight shot from the gates to the Castle. If the streets up on the Royal

Mile were similar to those where her community lay, there'd be plenty of dark alleys, closes, doorways and crevices in which to hide in the darkness if needed.

As she reached the gates Alys slipped her pair of blunted Sai from their sheaths on the sides of her thighs. Rotating them she held her Sai handles out with her grip on the cross bar and the main shaft running tight along her inside forearms. In this grip, the Sai were excellent for defence and attack. She left the third of her Sai in her belt. The sharpened edges and point made it her most lethal and least-used option. The Ringed and living people alike could easily be silenced or stunned with her more traditionally blunt Sai.

After checking along the fence-line where Bank Street met High Street, the boundary between The Brotherhood's territory and her own people's and the place she'd first met the boy with the bow, Alys picked the gate's lock and slipped through. A gust of wind shot along the length of High Street as she stepped through the gate, taking her breath away and causing her to retract through the gate in response.

Get a grip. She stepped back out onto the cobbles of The Royal Mile. Locking the gate behind her, Alys moved quickly and quietly along the sides of buildings, pupils wide, taking in every speck of available light and every detail of the unfamiliar street and buildings. Looking to her left, towards The Brotherhood's home at Mary King's Close, Alys' eyes were drawn to the gothic St Giles Cathedral. She made herself a silent promise to come back another time and investigate the beautiful building and its surrounding courtyards. Turning her attention to her right, she made her way up the cobbled Lawnmarket towards the Castle Esplanade.

As she forked right up to Castlehill, Alys noticed one of The Ringed stuck behind the railings of the fence around The Hub, another gothic-looking building. Trapped between the railings, arm broken and twisted around the fence, it was no threat to her. Trained to calculate risk, she decided not to waste energy silencing it and continued up Castlehill.

As she passed the railing, the former woman in a tattered red waitress uniform, craned its neck and snapped its jaws reflexively at her. A pitiful, dry groan escaped its throat. Alys looked at it for a second, taking in its appearance. In the advanced stages of decomposition – as advanced as these creatures got at any rate – the creature looked dry and broken. It creaked when it moved and carried dust, probably desiccated flesh, all over its person. The eyes were long gone having passed the putrefaction stage many years past, but it sensed her by some other means and turned its empty eye sockets towards her, repeating its weak, hungry groan.

Alys sighed, walked around the fence and quickly silenced the trapped ex-person, before moving up the slippery cobbled road once again towards the Castle.

Upon reaching the top of Castlehill the narrow, gothic street suddenly widened into a broad esplanade at the top of which stood Edinburgh Castle. Despite the freezing rain and the wind, and her own stoic disposition, Alys smiled to herself and began to walk out into the open space.

As she made her way across the square, she heard someone's boots running up Castlehill behind her. After vaulting over the railings on her right, Alys took position behind a large stone Celtic cross and sat silently watching as the boy with the bow appeared. Obviously in a state of panic, he carried his bow out in front, arrow in position, and a rucksack on his back. Scanning the Esplanade, he made his way carefully towards a massive arched door at the Castle. From where she sat Alys could see him retrieve a small object from behind one of the walls by the Castle, slip it in his bag and move back around the Esplanade towards Castlehill.

He stationed himself tucked in behind a wall, alert and watching, down the cobbled road that led to Mary King's Close. Clearly he expected someone. Alys slid silently around the perimeter of the fence she'd taken cover behind, her eyes never once leaving him until she could see part way down Castlehill in the direction he was facing.

An hour passed, during which time he kept his arrow loaded and his bow-string taut. There was no sign of movement in his muscles despite the tension in the bow for the whole of the hour he stood watch. It was a striking feat of stamina and strength. Alice was reluctantly impressed. Eventually, he decided that whoever he thought was coming after him was gone or had never come. Unhooking his arrow he sat on the wet cobbles, rucksack pressed up against the wall, visibly relieved and obviously defeated.

Part of Alys enjoyed seeing the carefree boy so visibly distraught, but most of her was crushed that the illusions she'd crafted for herself of his perfect, free life were just that, illusions. Unwilling to break the silence or his moment of reflection, she sat as still as the stone cross behind her watching his shoulders move in time with his sobs. Shame rose in her; she wanted to leave, to give the boy his privacy, but she stayed where she was.

The sound of breaking wood brought her instantly to full alert. She sprang to her feet, giving her position away to the boy who'd already risen and was turning his body side-on to her and taking aim. She froze. Not out of fear for herself – she'd looked this boy in the eye as a ten-year-old and knew that, despite the anger, she felt towards him, the jealousy of a life she imagined that he had – this was a good person. He wouldn't fire at her.

She'd frozen in place because she'd spotted the source of the noise which had startled them both out of their hiding places. Six Ringed had crashed through the boarded-up shop front immediately next to where the boy had been resting his back against the stone walls. With his attention on Alys, the boy was unaware of the dead hands reaching out to him or the teeth snapping in anticipation of a meal at last.

Her mother would look after herself and walk away. That's what Alys been taught to do and it was what she wanted to do. She pushed her mother's voice away and shouted at him.

"RINGED. BEHIND YOU."

Alys began running in his direction as she drew her Sai. Never taking her eyes from him, she saw realisation dawn in his green eyes and watched him swing around, turning his bow arm to bring it horizontal and smashing into the side of the nearest creature's temple. As she covered the ground between them, she saw him take a single step forward and kick another of The Ringed across its knee, causing the weak ligaments to snap and the creature to tumble forward.

He was quick and inventive but he'd obviously never fought a crowd before and was trying to fight them one at a time, as if they'd form an orderly queue and politely wait their turn. Inexperience was going to get him killed, or worse, get him bitten.

Alys threw herself into a high somersault, clearing his head as the downed creature dragged the boy to the ground with it. As she passed over the boy, she saw The Ringed using its arms to crawl up the prone boy, forcing him to jam his bow riser into its rotting mouth. She heard teeth crunch and a scream as she cleared the pair and flashed out a kick to a female creature's chest, knocking her over.

Silencing her with a Sai point to the temple, Alys rotated both Sai and launched both hands forward delivering the flat Sai handles into the foreheads of the two Ringed currently reaching for her. Yanking the handles free she whipped around once more, using the length of her Sai to break the arm then leg then neck of the last one, before pushing a Sai edge through its ocular cavity, bringing it to a final silence. Leaving her Sai poking from its eye socket, she smoothly pulled her third Sai from her belt and launched herself at the boy.

He'd pushed The Ringed off him after catching the creature's mouth around his bow, but was pulling at a blood-stained glove. It had bitten him. He saw her move towards him and held his injured hand up to halt her.

"Wait…"

He didn't get to complete his sentence; she'd already delivered her blow.

"What the hell?" He'd been complaining at her for a while now as they walked downhill together towards the gates on Bank Street.

"It looked like you'd been bitten." She shrugged. "Amputation's the only way of stopping the infection spreading."

He scowled at her and looked back to the tip of his middle finger on his left hand, or at least at the empty space where the top half of the finger formerly resided now covered in a tight cotton bandage.

"It was just a pressure wound to the nail."

Alys shrugged again.

The boy with the bow and the missing finger stared a little more at the cauterised and bandaged wound on his shortened finger, before shifting his eyes to her face and offering her a wide grin.

"Well, a 'thank you' is in order I suppose." He jabbed what remained of his mid-digit into the air in an attempt at a rude gesture.

Despite herself and the situation, Alys laughed out loud. It felt good to laugh with him. She couldn't recall the last time something had made her smile.

"I'm Alys." She offered him her hand.

The boy with the bow smiled broadly at her and took her hand in his.

"Thank you, Alys, I'm Joey."

They stood for a few long seconds not letting go of each other's hand, until it became awkwardly obvious that they'd both held onto each other a little too long. Fortunately Joey had the perfect opportunity to break the connection as he noticed a cloaked, masked man making his way towards them from the direction of Mary King's Close.

Alys grabbed her Sai, noticing Joey bring his bow up into the ready position, despite the obvious pain in his hand. Her mother had told her often of how men were weak, and unreliable in that weakness, but Joey was anything but weak.

She let him step slightly ahead of her. It wasn't a defensive gesture, he wasn't being gallant; she might've taken another finger from him for that. Instead he'd taken the initiative, simply because his weapon had the longest range.

They instinctively parted from each other, sidestepping in either direction to flank the cobbled street. She liked this kid more and more; he thought like she did. *Give the enemy two targets to worry about instead of one.* Masking a smile that threatened to pop up on her face with a scowl, she shouted towards the advancing man.

"Step into the light."

She saw his head cock to the side, as if he'd been amused at her order, but he followed the instruction by leaving the shade of the buildings and stepping into the moonlight.

Dressed in leather boots, gloves, black denims and a leather duster coat, *not a cloak*, the figure also wore the long-beaked mask of a plague doctor. Alys recognised it from books she'd read in her childhood. The sight of it threatened to chill her muscles, to seize them up, but she pushed away the instinctive fear that the ancient image had brought and stepped closer to him. Joey followed her lead.

Closing the distance between them, she noted that he wore two long blades, one sheathed at each hip. The way he moved, like flowing silk, told her how dangerous he was. She heard Joey draw further on the bow. He was readying a shot, probably figuring that the man had gotten close enough. The creaking string caused the masked man to halt and spread his arms, palms open in a submissive gesture.

"Mask off. Now," Alys barked at him.

Joey pulled the last ounce of tension into his bow. Alys took a ready stance, both Sai raised. The masked man performed a strangely old-fashioned little bow to show that he would comply. The gesture did nothing to make either teenager relax.

Reaching up, he grabbed the long, hooked nose with one hand and unbuckled a leather strap behind his head.

"A little jumpy tonight, Joseph?" Padre Jock asked in wry amusement.

"You know this guy? Why didn't you say?" Alys was instantly suspicious of both males. *Had she wandered into a trap?* She rotated her hips and adjusted her feet slightly, almost imperceptibly but enough to enable her to defend an attack from either male. Her mother's voice mocked her.

Joey had seen or felt the subtle changes in her posture and lowered his bow, placing it on the ground in response.

"I do know him, sort of, but I've never seen him dressed like that."

"Aye," Jock interrupted. "Sorry about that."

Alys eyed them both. She felt at war with herself. Everything her mother and community had taught her told her not to trust anyone, especially not men, and most especially not men from The Brotherhood. Her mother had also taught her to listen to her instincts, to trust her inner voice and it told her to relax: to trust the boy with the bow and the green eyes. To trust Joey.

Keeping her Sai in her hands – *there was trust and there was stupidity* – Alys lowered her arms and stood in a more relaxed manner.

"What's the story with you guys then?"

Jock smiled warmly at her, causing Joey to throw him a puzzled expression.

"Just looking out for the lad. He's kind of burned his bridges back there." Jock jabbed a thumb over his shoulder indicating the entrance to Mary King's Close.

Joey smiled his agreement before asking, "What's happening down there? Did they send you to bring me back?"

Jock laughed outright at the question.

"Not exactly, son. I've no intention of taking you back there."

Alys watched the exchange.

"What makes you think I'll allow you to *take* me anywhere?" Joey asked, clearly irked at Jock's attempts to take charge of him. "What happened back there? Why haven't they come after me?" Joey had raised his bow once more, taking aim at Jock's chest.

Alys backed him up. It felt like the thing to do, even though her common sense told her to leave them to it.

Jock surprised them both by sitting on the cobbles, cross-legged. "I had a little chat with them, son."

"I'm not your bloody son!" Joey was starting to get angry at the old man's amusement. Alys didn't blame him; she thought the old guy was irritating too, but also kinda cool.

"You've never spoken to me, cared about me or even looked at me without scowling before today. Why the hell would I trust you? I'll ask one more time, Jock."

Joey took careful aim and put maximum tension into the bow.

"Tell me what happened back there."

He's gonna kill this old guy, Alys thought.

Jock stood again, placed his weapons on the cobbles and walked slowly towards Joey.

"I... persuaded them to let you go; to come with me, out there." Jock nodded to his left, towards the fence-line that marked the limits of The Brotherhood's territory. Alys watched Joey's eyes narrow in mistrust and confusion.

"I also reminded them who brought you to Mary King's Close in the first place."

Joey lowered his bow and shook his head. The tears had begun to track their way down his face.

"I reminded them who had fetched you from a pool of blood five yards from where your mother was being devoured by those *things* that they choose to worship. I reminded them that it was me who kept the most dangerous of the Children of Elisha from their gates in return for your safe shelter."

"Why now? You let me live there all this time, why now?" Joey had fallen to his knees and was looking up at the padre, eyes streaming with tears now.

Alys watched what look like shame pass across Jock's face.

"Because they had women amongst them, back then. Mothers. All I was then was a killer. A Zombie-hunter. I couldn't be a father. I couldn't have a baby to care for, I didn't know how."

"Coward," Joey screamed out at the old man, rushing towards him to strike his face. Jock caught him easily by the wrists and brought his face close to his.

Alys was stunned into inaction and stood passively beside them watching it all unfold. *What could she do or say, anyway?*

"I *was* a coward to leave you there for so long, in the arms of mad men," Jock told him gently. "That's why I stayed and watched over you. I hoped that you'd be smart enough, be brave enough, braver than me, to break their brainwashing. They were keeping you safe and fed; that is what was important. I waited for when you would want to be free. For the time when you could leave the fences and not just become food for The Ringed. I watched them try to break your spirit, to make you believe with your whole heart that their way was the right way, but you kept a part of yourself free from their influence. The free-running through the streets up on the surface, the visits to the Esplanade; you were becoming independent in thought and deed."

Joey was crying freely now in Jock's arms, both men on their knees. Alys looked away, but felt her eyes drawn back to them crouched together on the black, wet cobbles of the Royal Mile.

"I wanted to give up once, I got tired of fighting," Joey whispered through his tears. "And then my birthday came and my bow with it. That was you?"

Jock gave a curt nod.

"I've been so proud watching you master that weapon. I've no right to be, but I am. You're going to need it where we're going, son. If you'll come?"

Joey stood to look over the fence-line into the unknown part of the city. The Royal Mile and the underground town of The Brotherhood had been his entire world for fifteen years. Alys doubted that he could leave, that he'd even want to. She was desperate to leave her community's fenced-in Garden, but only when the time was right. This boy had guts and some skill but he was nowhere near the fighter that she was and she wasn't ready for that side of the fence yet, which meant that he certainly wasn't. If she could have asked him to come with her, she would have.

Suddenly Joey turned back to face Jock.

"My mother, who was she?"

Jock shook his head.

"I don't know, son. Here, come with me."

Alys followed along behind them as the padre led Joey along towards Mary King's Close. She busied herself scanning the side buildings for any more surprises. It had shocked her how... fresh The Ringed who'd attacked her and Joey had been. They still had muscle and were fairly co-ordinated in their movements. They also had speed and that meant that they'd only crossed over a few months before. That was very unusual this far into the city-centre. Most of the dead found within the boundaries of their communities had been *made* in those first few days, as Mary King's Close had been the epicentre of the outbreak.

As they reached Mary King's Close, Alys noted that the heavy doors leading down to the crypts were closed tightly, probably locked. Jock had been correct in his assertion that The Brotherhood didn't care about pursuing Joey. Jock came to a stop at the arches of the City Chambers. Entering the first archway, Jock stared at the cobbles and spoke softly, pulling Joey close to him as he spoke.

"This is where I found her, where I found you. She was in the last stages of labour and unable to mute the screams that brought you out onto these cobbled roads. The dead were many in those days and livelier than the ones we see so often now. Her screams, which should have signalled a new life for both of you, merely drew them to end hers. Perhaps they smelled the blood; there was enough of it. I was up there," Jock pointed up at the battlements above the archway. "I'd just returned from a hunt. The Brotherhood paid me in those days, with food and shelter. I was charged by the founding Brothers with secretly dispatching the liveliest of the Children of Elisha. It went against the dogma but the founders knew that they wouldn't be left alone by the most active dead, the freshest ones. Their *methods* didn't work on the fresh ones."

Jock squeezed Joey's shoulder, a gesture of reassurance and a question: *should I go on?*

Joey merely stared at the spot on the cobbles that Padre Jock had indicated.

Jock chose to continue.

"By the time I'd dropped down, she'd bitten through the cord that attached you to her and had hidden you in that doorway over there." Jock pointed into the darkness. "She ran from you. Blood left behind her like a trail of gruesome breadcrumbs for the dead who pursued. She led them from you. It was the bravest act I've ever witnessed, Joseph."

Joey cried freely again, absorbing the words. This time Alys did look away and gave him his dignity.

"There were an army of them, forming a wall between her and me, but she saw me and pointed to the doorway as her last conscious act. I found you there, Joseph, fresh from the womb, still steaming, covered in your mother's blood, lying in a puddle of it with a reflection of the moon beside you. You were silent. I couldn't believe how silent you were. As I picked you up, I noticed some of the Brothers standing in High Street. They'd stood passively and watched the whole event. They would've let their precious Children eat you both. I threatened them, made them bring me to Father Grayson and made my deal with them to care for you. It was the best that I could do, son."

Alys had heard enough. Departing, she sent a silent prayer to Joey. *Go with Jock. Don't ever come back.* And then she went home, content for the first time in years that it was where she belonged. For now.

Padre Jock's Journal

In the first few hours of the outbreak people just assumed that the stories of monsters emerging, rabid from the depths of Mary King's Close, couldn't be real. Most of us thought that a trusted face would appear on the news telling us that it was all an elaborate hoax. That someone like Dynamo, the magician, had pulled a *War of The Worlds* type of event. Obviously we were wrong.

The Ringed were all over the social networks and news channels, but we had become so numb to shock, so arrogant, we didn't really consider that any real harm would come to us. We were used to our illusions of control, sure of our place in the world and our right to those privileges we enjoyed but never appreciated. Most of us expected an announcement to be made on the news channels that it was all just some clever marketing stunt and barely looked up from our screens. Almost ubiquitously, the prevailing attitude was one of "Go back to your reality shows, PlayStations or TVs. Everything's fine." Then all at once, it wasn't confined to our screens. It was in our streets, in our homes, standing snarling at us in full glorious high-def.

Even then you could see the shock and puzzlement on people's faces as they watched the dead begin to bring down their neighbours, their family — hell, even their pets. Eventually it hit. *This is real. Run.*

I was thirty years old when the plague hit Edinburgh and had been a minister in the Royal Marines since I was sixteen. Padre Jock Stevenson. I'd spent the last three years based in Scotland and had come to Edinburgh for a weekend visit. Some timing, eh? I'd been up on the Royal Mile, doing all the tourist crap, taking tours, sightseeing, so I was at the epicentre of the outbreak. Twenty-four hours in, they cut the power, everything disappeared, the internet, television, cell phones radios; all gone. Everything electrical, dead. God knows what they were thinking.

On day two I was barricaded inside Canongate Kirk along with around a hundred other survivors. We fought hard to keep the Kirk free of the infected. We thought that if only we could hold out for long enough then the government would get control and rescue us. Two days later they sealed the city with all its residents inside their hastily-erected fences and left us to it.

Initially we kept hoping that the fences were temporary. They'd built them so quickly, it must have taken all of the armed services. Only they could have done such an effective job so speedily. We told each other that they'd come back. That our families on the outside would demand they came in to clear the dead and rescue the uninfected. We clung onto a lot of fantasies in those days.

As the weeks passed we became skilled foragers, leaving the safety of the Kirk at regular intervals and in teams, in search of food and supplies. We lost a lot of people in those early days, when the dead still moved so quickly; when they were still so fresh, so predatory.

After a year had passed, people had given up hope on ever communicating with the outside world again. Some thought that the plague must have escaped, despite the fences, and the rest of the country, maybe the world, was in the same position as we were. Some preached that we'd faced God's judgment for our consumerist ways, or His judgement of the gays, or whatever twisted notion they subscribed to. There was no shortage of doomsayers or bigots before the plague hit and the end of our city only strengthened those beliefs. Most of us suspected that we'd just been abandoned.

Whatever they believed, people did what people always do: they fought. They chose sides and they built more fences to found and segregate communities. I roamed around for a few years, always making my way back to the city-centre for long spells. At times I took payment from The Brotherhood for keeping their community free of all but the most decayed dead. Eventually I stopped travelling around and stayed permanently in the city-centre for fifteen years, watching over you, Joseph.

I met a lot of people. I killed a lot of people and ex-people to keep my little corner of the world safe. I existed instead of living, until the screams of a woman delivering her baby into this hell brought me running.

Three Years Later

North Edinburgh

2050

Chapter 5

Joey

"Again," Jock barked.

Joey sighed, but didn't argue and began repeating the series of exercises Jock had been teaching him. He made rotating movements of his legs over a short wall in a sweep across the wall; spin and repeat the process. The exercises Jock drilled him with were inventive, exhausting and hugely effective in developing the muscles he used when free-running through the city. Jock was a monumental pain in the ass and a hard task master but he knew how to get the best from a body.

"Good, another centimetre higher with that right calf on the sweep, Joseph."

Joey listened and concentrated, making the adjustments Jock suggested. He'd long ago learned to trust the padre's instructions.

In the three years since they'd left the only home Joey had ever known on the Royal Mile, Jock and he had ventured throughout most of north Edinburgh. Leaving the confines of the inner fences of the city-centre communities, they'd made their way to the outer fence-line, which ran along the city's north bypass, and had criss-crossed from Portobello to Corstorphine, traveling into the city and out to the fence periodically. They'd mapped most of the area and encountered many of the dead. Most of all, they'd talked and they'd trained together.

In Jock, Joey couldn't have found a more skilled mentor or a finer surrogate father. A far cry from the man he'd imagined him to be for so long, Jock seemed in his easy-going and positive attitude as happy to be free of the confines of the Royal Mile as Joey himself. As they'd travelled throughout the remains of the Edinburgh suburbs and districts, Jock had passed along lessons on survival, combat, navigation and strategy, all learned from his years as a Marine and decades as a Zombie-hunter on the Royal Mile.

They'd become a lethal team, co-ordinated in their movement through the streets they travelled and lethal in their precision in silencing The Ringed.

It had taken Joey a few weeks to get his head around silencing the dead. He'd been taught his whole life that the dead were to be revered, left to roam in peace, but long conversations with Jock and several dangerous encounters with the more aggressive, fresher dead had helped justify the silencing of the walking dead. Jock and he now saw this as a way of bringing the moving corpses to peace. To end their suffering.

The Ringed couldn't feel pain, as far as they could determine, but who knew what went on inside their brains, if anything? They simply had no way of knowing but genuinely felt that silencing the creatures was the safest thing for the survivors in the area, and it felt like the right thing to do.

Jock mostly used his dual blades, one in each hand facing in alternate directions. He'd aim to the temple, base of the skull or the eye. These were the three best places to penetrate the skull and sever the fragile connection needed to animate the body.

Joey had become a master with the bow. His own training regime had made him an excellent archer but Jock's input had turned him into an almost infallible marksman. He could accurately strike even fast moving targets from a range of fifty metres and from a crouched or a standing position. They'd practiced hand to hand combat together for thousands of hours and had hundreds of lightning-fast combat sequences at their disposal to disarm, maim and to kill the living or silence the dead.

They had a handful of pre-prepared, smooth tactics and strategies they used most often to dispatch The Ringed and code words for each of them to synchronise their attack or defence. More often than not, they favoured the Donald Duck. Joey wasn't sure where Jock had gotten his code names from but they were always a little silly. The Donald Duck involved Jock attracting the attention of the creature, whilst Joey crept behind and silenced it with a blade to the base of the skull. Very simple but effective.

In the last twelve months, they'd concentrated on teaching Joey to work with two blades. He was far from a natural with the weapons, but Jock insisted that he needed a close-range weapon for times when his bow wasn't a good option. Joey had argued that he would simply use his bow as a staff, but Jock had countered with a nod towards his missing middle finger, so knives it was. He'd never be any use in a knife fight against a highly-skilled living person, but had become confident enough to deal with The Ringed using them.

"Right, good work, wee man." Jock flung an arm around his charge and pulled him in for a one-armed hug. "Let's get something to eat and get our heads down for the night."

Still a little uncomfortable with Jock's warmth and easy affection, Joey patted the padre on the back and smiled.

"Right, old man. Soft play?" Joey asked.

"You saw that, did you?"

Joey had spotted the former pub with attached kid's play area as they'd trained. Clad in still-colourful padded mats, the soft play areas they frequently came across on their travels made for excellent accommodation. The play areas were normally in a fenced-off part of the building and padded to a greater comfort level than the back of a car, their usual camping choice.

"Yeah, I'll go do a quick check around the building. You want to get inside?"

Jock raised his eyes to survey the coming storm clouds. "Good idea," he smiled, subconsciously rubbing at his arthritic right shoulder. "I'll get the rabbit on, son. Be careful."

Nodding in reply, Joey did a quick check that his bow and his knives were primed and his boots laced tightly. He pulled his hood up far enough to shelter him but not obscure his peripheral vision. The checks were automatic after years of being on the road with Jock. The padre had stopped needing to remind him of these precautions months back.

Fully prepared, Joey watched Jock retreat into the pub, knife in each hand. Jock would do a sweep of the building interior before setting up their sleeping area and cooking the game they'd trapped earlier in the day. One thing they were never short of out in the suburban expanse between inner and outer fences was rabbits. The local woodland wildlife had taken the absence of humans as their cue to colonise former homes, gardens, schools and anywhere else they could feed, breed and avoid the dead. The abundance of food was something that Joey hadn't expected when they'd crossed the fence-line of The Brotherhood three years previously.

Jock had taught him everything he knew about survival in the no man's land the two of them had spent their days, weeks, months and years exploring. Food, water, and shelter had become easy to find for the pair, but still they roamed looking for who knows what. They were living: not surviving, *living*. They'd met people, some good, some not so good. Occasionally they helped people out, sometimes they even had some fun. Joey had never expected to be so happy, so free.

Supressing a smile, Joey focused on stalking the perimeter of the building. As he moved silently along, staying close to the moss and lichen-covered walls, periodically he'd reach out three feet or so, stick a little tent peg into the ground and wind some cat gut around it, stretching it along to the next peg and the next until the building's perimeter was surrounded by a line of cat gut with little bells at regular intervals. This was a first-warning device they'd cobbled together from fishing line and those wee bells that were once found in budgie's cages which they'd scavenged from various shops on their travels. The cat gut was very difficult for the living to see and The Ringed rarely fixed their sight on anything except a meal, so it provided an effective warning device.

He and Jock were always assessing and reassessing which items were vital in their respective rucksacks. Camping and mountaineering stores on Rose Street had provided them with outdoor clothes in the first days after their departure from The Close. Joey still enjoyed the comfort of dressing in his black denims and hiking boots, but he'd traded his battered old boots for a more practical pair of Berghuas walking boots. Both had scavenged base layers, waterproofs and jackets, Joey taking a leather jacket with windproof inner layer that Jock had cursed the store for not having in his size. The leather was perfect for allowing free movement but gave none of the swooshing, rubbing noise of some of the man-made waterproof jackets.

It was a constant battle, choosing between what was essential and what wasn't; which items were worth each of them carrying, in case they were separated, and which it was a waste of energy to duplicate. They both carried the items they agreed that they couldn't do without and personal preferences guided their decisions for the rest.

The only exception was the pouch of Carrionite Joey had scooped up on his hurried departure from The

Close, which still lay at the bottom of the rucksack. Why he'd chosen to keep the substance, Joey couldn't say.

Completing his sweep, Joey returned to the pub's entrance, closed and barricaded the door behind him, and walked towards the flickering lights of Jock's fire at the rear of the large room. Noticing a few of The Ringed with damaged temples, he assumed correctly that Jock had silenced them. Crouching, he stole a quick glance at the condition of them. They were pretty old and decayed. Mostly dried out, they'd reached that point in the decomposition process where the decay seemed to halt. It was one of those unexplained things they'd noticed on their travels. The creatures would decay to a certain point and then remain in that state. It made it very difficult to guess when the person had died. With Ringed like these ones, usually the best sign of when they'd turned were the clothes they wore. These two were dressed in the striped uniforms of soft-play attendants, with plastic *My name is John, My name is Evie* badges still visible amongst the rags.

Mostly they'd encountered newly-dead out in no man's land. Lots of children. Joey couldn't get his head around why anyone would choose to bring a baby into this world but obviously plenty of them had. *His own mother had*. Pushing the thought away, he noticed the smell of rabbit cooking and continued along to the soft play area.

"You enjoy that, son?" Jock nodded at the small pile of bones beside Joey, picked clean of all traces of muscle.

"Yeah. You do the best rabbit, Jock. Will have to get you to teach me."

Jock grinned. "Aye, that'd mean you actually cooking once in a while, Joseph."

"I caught it," Joey shrugged. Then he asked, "Jock? When are we going to head south?"

Jock ignored him and gnawed on a femur, tearing the last little strips of thigh off.

Joey had brought up the possibility of returning to the city-centre and continuing on to the city's south side several times over the last few weeks but Jock had been cold on the idea, brushing him off with reasons to stay in the northern suburbs. Joey decided to push a little harder this time.

"I think that it's worth the journey. We can check in with The Brothers, make sure they're managing all right without you keeping the faster Ringed limited. After that, we can explore the southern fence-line and zig-zag our way across the suburbs."

"No," said Jock, cutting off the next justification from Joey before he could offer it.

Joey quickly hid the anger that had flashed before Jock could see it. Not that there was much danger of him noticing, he hadn't looked up once. Jock's manner reminded Joey of the old Jock; the scowling creep who'd skulk around the Royal Mile, watching him. Watching over him as it had turned out. Lightening his tone, attempting something between cheeriness and seriousness, Joey continued.

"We could see Alys for a while too. Pass on some of the things we've learned out here. We do owe her, Jock. I owe her."

Jock threw the bone he'd been working on into the fire. As he looked at Joey the fire between them danced in his eyes.

"I've been south before, Joseph. Bad…"

Jock stopped for a second and massaged his closed eyelids with his index fingers. When he looked up, he'd decided what to say.

"Bad people live there."

Joey relaxed, confident that he could now convince Jock to go south.

"So what? There are bad people everywhere. We've done a pretty good job of avoiding them or chasing them away so far. We're a great team, Jock."

Shaking his head, Jock continued. "We… you've never met people like these. I'm not taking you anywhere near them. *I* don't want to be anywhere near them."

Joey had never heard Jock speak this way before. The padre was confidence and practicality personified. This just wasn't him.

Joey stayed quiet for a few long moments. "Where are they, Jock? You know you'll have to tell me."

Jock had made a point over the years of reinforcing Joey with the notion that he wouldn't be there for much longer to teach him how to survive; that he had to absorb as much as possible and learn the territory well enough to allow him to make a life, a safe life, when Jock was gone. "I'm nearly seventy, Joseph," he'd say. "That's an old man in this new world ruled by the dead." Joey would laugh to lighten the mood and tell him he had plenty years left, but they both knew that it was wishful thinking.

The scavenging, the constant travelling, the fighting and the presence of sickness all around were aging him. He was slower, clumsy at times; he was getting forgetful and making mistakes. He was a young man trapped in an old man's body and that body was beginning to fail him.

Jock considered the man Joey was becoming and knew that the kid would go south on his own once he'd passed on. He couldn't let him go there blind of the dangers. Jock let out a long sigh.

"He calls himself Somna, thinks that he's some sort of messenger from God."

Joey leaned in closer to the fire, giving Jock his full attention.

"He…" Jock searched for the word, "worships, I suppose. He worships one of The Ringed, a man that used to be a celebrity."

Seeing a look of confusion flash across Joey's face, Jock explained.

"Celebrities were people who'd gotten famous for something; like an achievement of some kind or a skill, or just by being on TV. You remember I told you about TV?"

Joey nodded.

"Well, he's got this Ringed who used to be a famous footballer. It's in a pretty advanced stage, like those ones out there." Jock indicated John and Evie out in the hall. "So he has this footballer who was a big hero to him when he was a kid, one of the most famous. This footballer was global. His face was everywhere, advertising all sorts of products. He had soccer academies and what-not as well, as I recall. Well, Somna, he… talks to him. Receives commands from this rotted corpse of a once famous athlete who'd been unlucky enough to be attending a fashion show in Edinburgh when the plague broke." Jock raised his eyebrows, acknowledging how crazy it sounded.

"So, he's just like that nutter we came across in Pilton. Him with the panda," Joey laughed.

Jock snapped at him "No. He's not like that man."

Embarrassed at his own outburst he sat himself back down.

"This man believes that it's his mission to rid Edinburgh of the living. He thinks that the dead footballer has chosen him to do this. He and his men have killed dozens of people who are simply trying to survive this mess. Maybe hundreds"

"Okay," said Joey, palms in a submissive gesture to calm the padre. "Where exactly is he?"

Jock eyed him suspiciously. "You're never to go there, you understand?"

Joey nodded.

"This isn't something we can change or can help with. He has hundreds, maybe a thousand, dedicated to his cause and he collects more followers from the communities he destroys in his king's name. If we go south, we stay away from the fence-line. Somna and his people, they call themselves The Exalted. They think that anyone who survived in the city-centre is now dead as it was the epicentre of the outbreak. That's the only reason that they haven't made their way to the city-centre communities – that and the fact that they've been busy torturing, killing, *purifying* they call it, their way across the towns south of the city."

Jock looked crushed as he relayed the story.

"You've met them." It wasn't a question.

Jock gave an almost imperceptible nod of his head.

"I tried to stop a small group of them from killing a young couple out in Liberton. Obviously I failed. They tortured those people, cut parts from them and took joy, actual joy, from doing so. They fed the body parts to their king and left those kids in pieces to rot. Just for being in their path, for being alive. I barely escaped. You must never go near them, you hear me, Joseph. I'm telling you where they are so that you can avoid it."

"I promise, Jock." Joey meant it.

The padre spent the next thirty minutes describing the location and layout of The Exalted tribe's camp in Drum Woods. Then he added, "There have been rumours of a cure for the infection, you know. In the old Royal Infirmary out on Little France on the South Side."

Joey nodded. Despite never having explored the south, Jock had insisted that he spend hours studying maps of Edinburgh they'd found in petrol stations and hotels over the years. They'd adapted a map of the city complete with all the fenced communities they'd learned of on their trips and some Jock had encountered in the south, fences and

dEaDINBURGH: Vantage • 77

gates marked off in brightly fluorescent highlighter ink. They heard a lot of stories from other travellers.

"It's bull," Jock told him. "At least I believe that the rumour's a lie, told by The Exalted and spread to lure more victims to the south."

Joey walked around to where Jock sat. "If I go without you, I'll be careful. No heroics."

"No heroics," Jock repeated. It was a phrase he'd drilled into Joey that'd become a symbol of their relationship. The secrets they'd shared, hopes for the future and lessons they'd learned from each other. It had become their motto. *All heroes die, son. Don't be a hero, be a survivor.*

As Jock opened his mouth to continue talking, a tinkling sound from outside the building brought their weapons to their hands and both men to their feet.

Silently, they took flanking positions in view of the only entrance. The door's handle started to dip down. *It's not one of The Ringed,* Joey thought. *They don't open doors, or can't.* Darting his eyes to Jock he acknowledged that Jock had seen the movement and that the padre would change strategy in response.

He put his blades away and pulled his bow up into the ready position, waiting for whoever came through. Jock disappeared completely from sight. Joey knew from experience that his mentor would reappear when the time was right.

"Just come through," he shouted at the door. "I won't shoot."

A few beats of silence followed before a man's voice with a clipped, upper-class English accent replied.

"You have a gun. That's very unusual. Can I see it?"

Joey ignored the odd question.

"Step through slowly."

"Thank you, I'd love to share dinner, very kind of you to ask."

Great, thought Joey, *another nutter. With any luck he won't have dragged any animals out of the zoo along with him.*

Stepping through the door, Joey noted that the man, despite his amused tone and breezy affectation, kept part of his body behind the door, giving himself a partial shield. This confirmed for Joey that despite his almost bizarre appearance and manner, he was not a fool.

Tall, maybe six-two, he had a lean, muscular build. Red hair fell long over his forehead and partly over his eyes, and a neatly-trimmed but longish beard framed his face. With all the slightly-greying red hair it was difficult to make out any of his features distinctly. Joey guessed that he might be in his mid-fifties or older.

What he'd dressed in couldn't be more out of place in the dead city of Edinburgh; that was probably the point. The man wore the jacket, trousers, spiked shoes and hat of a golfer. Down to the single gloved hand holding a nine iron he was the perfect image of a man out playing a round. Looking around the dark interior as he poked half his body through, he spotted Joey, bow arm extended, string drawn, and greeted him like an old friend.

"Oh! It's a bow. How perfectly wonderful."

He immediately entered the room fully, leaving the cover he'd had behind the door. Arm extended, hand offered for a gentlemanly shake, he strode over to Joey who remained as still as rock and as friendly as one. When he reached within three feet of an immovable and unfazed Joey, Jock flashed out from a hidden alcove on the man's right and pressed one of his knives to the man's throat, the other to his genitals.

"That's far enough," Jock growled, in what he'd once told Joey was his 'Batman voice'. The reference, as usual, was lost on Joey.

"Drop the club." Jock motioned at the man's hand.

"Oh, wonderful, simply wonderful luck. There are two of you," exclaimed the man positively thrilled to be held at the end of Jock's knives. "How lovely to meet y…"

Jock pressed his blade in against his throat, cutting him off, clearly not buying the man's cheery demeanour.

"Drop the blade," Jock whispered this time, "last warning."

Joey took final aim and prepared to release if and when Jock dropped his shoulder, giving him the shot.

The stranger didn't bother to talk or smile this time. He simply dropped his club as requested, waited for the infinitesimal withdrawal of Jock's blade and then flashed his own very small, very pointed stiletto blade out from nowhere up to and into Jock's carotid artery.

Spinning Jock around with his left arm hooked over the older man's chest, he faced Jock toward Joey whilst keeping the blade lodged in Jock's neck. Joey's eyes never left the blade. It didn't budge a centimetre despite him manhandling Jock. Instantly the man's tone changed to pure reptile as he addressed Joey.

"Okay, young man. The situation is thus. I have your... father?" He stole a quick glance at Jock. "Whatever he is to you, I have him positioned just so." He made an almost imperceptible little movement of his eyes, motioning to the dagger. "If I remove this blade, the old minister here will give this lovely public house a new coat of paint. A badly needed new coat of paint, if you don't mind me saying. It's terribly dreary in here." He laughed at his own joke.

Still smiling his crocodilian smile, he continued. "I'm willing to gamble that you don't have the skills to repair this wound before he bleeds out."

Something Joey did, although he'd swear he hadn't reacted, told the man that he was right.

"Ah, good," he said. "I'm also willing to gamble that you're nowhere near so effective with those blades on your waist as you clearly are with that bow. That rigid arm of yours tells me how much you practice with that lovely weapon."

Joey stood completely still, focusing on his target but not daring to take the shot. Despite his stoic exterior, the man clearly received some subconscious reply in a small gesture from him.

"Excellent. Now, I want you to know that I'm not here to take anything from you." He glanced at the knife at Jock's artery in emphasis. "I simply knocked to see if there was any space at the table, so to speak."

Joey remained in place, mind racing.

"Here's how it can play out, young man. You can take that shot you have aimed at my right eye. I have no doubt that you'll kill me instantly as I can see how talented you are. But my gamble, remember, is that you won't do that, because then he'll die, won't he?"

Joey threw his bow to the carpet and pulled his blades free, taking his ready stance.

The man smiled. "We could do it that way, but you've already seen how fast I am, haven't you. You already know how that will end." The man spoke so gently; he'd slipped into the cheery English gent voice again.

"Let's do it my way. Your role is to back all the way up to the bar over there. Keep your knives if you wish, it makes no difference. Once your back touches the bar, I'm going to take my dagger out of the minister's neck. When that happens his blood will spray the wall over there." He nodded at a mirrored wall to his right. "Probably ruin that nice white dog-collar."

He smiled at his own joke once again, making Joey hate him.

"You'll want to run to your minister, but don't. If you do, you'll only get in the way of what I have to do to stop him from dying. And I will stop him from dying."

To emphasise his intention, he unhooked his left arm from around Jock and slipped a first aid kit from his bag.

"Once he's all patched up, I know that it'll be difficult for us to be friends now, but that's what's going to happen. He'll have lost some blood and he'll be weak for a few days. I don't wish to be rude, young man, but you simply cannot beat me on your own. Let's spend the night talking, sharing that lovely meat and these comfortable surroundings and we can part ways in the morning. Deal?"

Joey looked at Jock whose face was as calm as ever. He blinked once for yes, their agreed-upon silent communication.

"Okay," said Joey, forcing his voice to be steady, deeper than his tight throat should have been capable of.

"Excellent decision."

He beamed and immediately lowered Jock to the carpet face down. With his left hand, he deftly pulled several objects that Joey couldn't identify in the darkness from his kit, pulled his dagger from Jock's neck, moving aside a little to avoid the spray, and stuck his thumb in the hole. After five minutes, Jock was sitting, drinking from a water canteen, face full of colour again and warily listening to his attacker/saviour chatter like an excited kid on Christmas Eve.

He introduced himself as Bracha; just Bracha, no first name. Apparently in his early twenties and living in Stockbridge when the plague struck, he'd been in the city with some friends, visiting from London.

He talked for hours about cars.

"Can't get them working as the petrol has turned to varnish, unless it's a sealed container, in the dark, underground, like a fuel station, but of course we'd need power to get it out. Diesel's even worse; diesel bugs eat it, y'see. Nasty little creatures, a bacteria that feeds on diesel, amazing, quite amazing."

He continued, unfazed by the chilly company, jabbering at machine-gun rate about food resources, people he'd met and a dozen other topics. According to Bracha, he had lots of friends. "I make friends everywhere I travel, just one of those people. Always been a people person."

"Friends? Like *we* are your friends?" Jock had asked him.

The excitable boy disappeared and the reptilian man slid out for a second.

"Oh, no. Some have been very close friends."

Suddenly he snapped back to the cheery Bracha, everyone's friend.

"How rude of me, I've hardly let you say a word."

As the evening wore on, they relaxed a tiny amount and gave Bracha the briefest details of their home community up on the Royal Mile, exaggerating the defences to discourage the man from visiting. He seemed particularly interested that the neighbouring community was comprised wholly of females. Joey was quick to point out how skilled the women were in combat.

Eventually Bracha gave out an exaggerated and highly animated yawn, stretched himself out on some foam shapes and lay down for the night. Jock nodded to the door, signalling that Joey should follow him outside.

"I'm going to kill this guy, Joseph."

"Why? I know he's a bit creepy, but he did patch you up and I did threaten him first."

Jock wasn't for discussing the issue. "I've met men like this before, in the forces. He's dangerous."

"So are we in the right circumstances. Anyone who has survived in this city is dangerous or they'd be shuffling around with the rest of The Ringed," Joey replied.

Jock looked sadly at him for a second.

"Okay. Go get your things, we're leaving. We'll put as much distance between us and him as we can overnight. Once we're confident that we've lost him, we can set up camp and rest for a few days."

Joey grimaced at the thought of leaving the comfortable building for a night on the road.

"It's that or kill him," Jock said flatly.

Joey huffed and went back inside for his rucksack. He hadn't had the chance to unpack it, so it saved him the job of repacking now.

By morning, they'd made their way out to the Gyle Shopping Centre.

"Let's keep pushing on," Jock had insisted.

Spending the day working their way through Sighthill and another night working their way back on themselves to Murrayfield, they found a PC World building and made camp. Confident that their long trip had left Bracha far behind they fell into a deep sleep.

Morning brought a wonderful golden light through the office window where they'd slept. It fell on Joey's sleeping face, gently warming him for an hour before he sensed it and woke.

"Oh, man I needed that." He smiled over at Jock. His smile vanished the instant he saw the padre.

Jock was already awake, eyes wide open in quiet horror, staring at the ceiling. He had his index finger in the reopened hole in his neck and was sweating profusely with the effort he was employing to stay still.

"Jock!"

Joey stood over his best friend willing a solution to come to him. As he scanned Jock he noticed that a pool of blood had formed around and under him – a massive pool – that'd gone straight under the pallet Joey had slept on. The office floor was an inch deep in Jock's blood. Despite the finger in his artery, Jock had slowly bled out. He was dying.

"Joseph. Bracha. In the night," Jock croaked, voice as dry as one of *theirs*. "Bring my satchel," he said weakly.

"What good's a bloody Bible going to do?" Joey screeched at him in panic.

Jock tried to speak again, but couldn't and pointed again at his bag.

Fetching the leather satchel, Joey paused for a split-second before opening it. In all their travels, moments of danger, heart to hearts and secrets they'd shared, Jock had never once mentioned the contents of this bag and Joey had never asked. At times he'd been desperate to know what it contained, and why of all Jock's possessions it was the first he checked, the most important to the man. Yesterday he'd have given anything to know; today, he wished he wasn't about to find out.

Reaching in, Joey's fingers found the binding of a very thick leather-bound book. Pulling it out, he handed it to Jock without so much as glancing at the cover. It felt like a betrayal to look at it.

"Take it. It's yours now. It'll tell you everything I've done, everything I've learned."

Looking down at the book that Jock had shoved back to him, he smoothed one hand over the surface of the cover before opening it to scan the title page. He couldn't read the words, he'd never learned to read; few in The Brotherhood had.

It wasn't a Bible, not even close. It was Jock's journal, the story of the man's life. He hugged it close to his chest and promised Jock he'd take care of it.

"You have to find a way to read this, Joseph. It's important." A violent spasm made him stiffen for a few seconds. Joey watched him accept the pain, absorb it and compose himself once more.

"More." Jock pointed at the bag.

Joey stuck his hand in and pulled out a rubbery-feeling block. He noticed a seam and pulled, causing a lid to pop off and expose a metal rectangular end. Joey didn't have a clue what it was.

"Flash… It's a flash-drive. It stores information. You need a computer to see what's on it."

"What is this, Jock? What's on it?"

"It was *hers*. She threw it to me as they took her life. I don't know what's on it, but she wanted you to have it. I really believe that."

A painful cough suddenly racked Jock's body. His finger fell away from his throat where it had been held for who knew how long.

"Her name was Michelle. Michelle MacLeod, your mother. She wasn't from here, Joseph. The way she was dressed, the way she spoke, it was all wrong." Jock whispered the words. Pain, emotional not just physical, screamed in his eyes. "Someone put her in here, from outside."

Stunned, Joey was caught between the elation that he knew his mother's name and had been given a gift from her, and the pain of losing his best friend. That his mother had come from the outside world barely registered in the whirlwind he was caught in.

He searched his mind for something he could do, something that he could say... anything. Suddenly he stopped trying and just looked at Jock's pale, drained face.

Taking his hand he kissed Jock softly on the lips and thanked him for being his best friend, his brother and his father, in deed if not in fact. Finally he said goodbye to the only person who'd ever loved him.

When the morning came he buried the man who had taught him to survive and said a final goodbye, placing the last item he'd found in the bag gently against Jock's grave. Before picking up the clumsy trail that Bracha had left and setting off towards Princes Street Gardens, he glanced back for a final look at Jock's resting place. Throwing a blown kiss at the broken framed photograph that glinted in the sun of a young Jock in uniform, arm around his wife and two sons, he whispered, "Thank you, Jock. Rest easy."

Then he set off after Bracha and towards Alys, the only other living person he knew or gave a damn for.

Chapter 6

Alys

Saint Thomas of Aquin's High School Reception Office

"Go to sleep, Stephanie. We have an early start in the morning."

"Can't," Stephanie replied huffily. "Too much going on."

She pointed a finger up at her temple.

Alys understood. This was her little cousin's first trip away from the confines of The Gardens. It had taken them two days to reach the little safe-haven that Alys had set up in the former High School's office on a previous trip, but the journey time had done little to dampen Steph's excitement, or slow down the torrent of questions she fired.

Alys was glad that she'd decided to bring her cousin this particular route. She'd travelled it dozens of times since she'd been made a Ranger and permitted to leave the fences of The Gardens by her mother. She knew the area's safe places and she knew which places were best avoided. Most of The Ringed in this part of the city were *old*. Slow and severely decayed, one simply had to keep away from them for the most part. She knew a few of the survivors in the area also, forming loose friendships with some of the younger ones. She stayed clear of the others and they reciprocated. All in all it was a good section to bring Steph out to for her first trip.

What her journey with her cousin had taught her so far was that the younger girl simply wasn't ready to be outside of The Gardens' fences. Steph was too loud, too clumsy, too trusting of others to make for a good Ranger. She couldn't pay attention to the simplest instruction and walked along completely oblivious to the many useful items, signs or places they passed. Of course this meant that the kid was oblivious to the dangers also. Essentially Steph treated being in the larger area of the inner fence that circled around Princes Street, down Lothian Road and along Clerk Street and The Bridges like a holiday outing rather than the precarious exercise in scavenging, mapping and networking that it was.

They'd be travelling home by a more direct route tomorrow.

It wasn't Steph's fault that she was so flippant in her approach to life. Steph's mother, Alys' Aunt Fiona, hadn't included her in Jennifer's survival programme. Fiona firmly believed that children should be children and run and play whilst they still wanted to. Her sister, of course, disagreed and had convinced all of the women in The Gardens that the days when kids could be free and innocent, protected from life's hardships, had died with the city and left with the men. She convinced all but her own sister to enrol their children in her programme, but had succeeded in enrolling Steph in combat class in which she was at best a middling student.

Time had proven Jennifer correct in her strategy. The Gardens was a thriving community of women and a few young men, who'd been children of its first inhabitants, able to fend and provide for themselves. They were also more than able to defend themselves thanks to Jennifer's foresight.

A spirited twenty-year-old when the plague-ridden corpses of Mary King's Close had been released from their four-hundred-year entrapment, Jennifer Shephard had pulled and dragged her younger sister through the streets of Edinburgh. Moving them from group to group, Jennifer latched on to the most able people, the ones who would not only protect the girls but who could teach them to survive. Ex-soldiers, police officers and outdoors-types were made use of, drained of all they could teach and dumped for the next most useful category.

Right from the outbreak Jennifer hadn't expected to be rescued from the dead city and set about her single-minded mission to learn what she could to survive, to fight. By the time her group had colonised The Gardens some ten years later, Jennifer was a fearsome, if inflexible, leader determined to protect everyone she travelled with.

Alys wasn't sure when, why or how Jennifer had driven the men out. She'd heard stories from some of the older women who'd travelled with the Shephard sisters in the early days about rapes and sexual bullying. She'd heard that the men took what they wanted, in return for their 'protection'. They'd apparently thought themselves in charge due to their perceived strength. Alys had heard that her mother had shown them what real strength was.

She had no idea why her father had left along with the rest of the men and simply had to accept that her mother must have had a good reason for banishing them. Maybe she didn't have a choice. It was all just rumour and hearsay. Alys had given up asking Jennifer years ago about her father or any of the other men. Jennifer simply wouldn't tell her anything, other than that they were safer this way. Stronger.

It was hard to argue with that. In the time she'd been a Ranger, Alys had encountered dozens of communities, established within the large inner fence. They ranged from a handful of strangers banded together and living in buildings, including the basement flats of the many townhouses, to whole families who'd joined other families and formed fenced-in communities not unlike the one at The Gardens. Some were religious, some purely pragmatic. Some had theories on why Edinburgh had been abandoned, but most didn't care and were just trying to survive another day. None of the communities had the resources, organisation or safety of The Gardens, or even The Brotherhood.

Just thinking of The Brotherhood brought an image of Joey to her mind's eye. She hadn't seen him once in the years since she'd walked away and left him and Jock on The Royal Mile mourning the mother he'd never known. However, she'd heard stories about an old minister and a young man with a bow from some other travellers in the inner fence. It seemed that they spent their time travelling the north of the city. The people she'd met said only good things about them. A man she'd encountered in The Meadows, a former supermarket manager with whom she'd shared a fire and a meal, had told her that the padre and the boy had saved him from a group of Ringed, "the fresher ones," he'd told her. They wouldn't accept anything in return for their assistance, but had sent him in the direction of some food stashes they kept throughout their routes. According to the supermarket manager, they did this regularly for people in the north.

She'd met a woman who'd also spoken to them. The woman had been walking towards trouble, something about a maniac with zoo animals, and the pair had turned her onto a different route around where the man made his home. She'd described Joey as handsome, with blond hair, the greenest of eyes and a bow. The woman thought it amazing that someone had taken time to help her. "So few do, love," she'd said.

Alys' heart swelled when she heard that they were safe, that they were the good people she'd taken them for. This was the one instance in which she'd disobeyed her mother and the one instance when her mother had been wrong. Some men *could* be trusted. Alys sighed, brushed Steph's hair over her right ear with her finger and told the twelve-year-old to go to sleep again.

Walking outside onto Chalmers Street, Alys looked up at the clear night sky and wondered if the stars had been so visible back when the city had been alive. Had people even noticed them if they were? Mum said that the people of old Edinburgh were worse than the ones who lived here now. "Self-absorbed," she'd called them many times. "Always in a rush, always too important to talk." According to her mum many people were like that in the old days: living, but not really living; focused on shit that didn't matter. Alys never really understood what she was referring to but had nodded along in agreement to keep the peace.

After a final check around the front of the building, Alys made her way back inside, barricaded the office door and lay beside her cousin. As she drifted off to sleep, she wondered if Joey looked at the stars. She decided that he did; he'd been underground for so long, he'd appreciate them more than most. Alys had thought back to the night she'd met Joey and Jock many times in the three years since, replaying the events frame by frame in her mind's eye. No matter how many times she scanned the images, she couldn't pinpoint the exact moment that she'd chosen to trust the boy with the bow; when she'd stopped resenting his *freedom* and began to see him for who he was – someone as trapped as she'd been at the time.

Sometimes, when she thought of him, she wished that she'd taken him to The Gardens, but Jennifer would have sent him packing, or worse. She'd spent hours examining that day, trying to decide why she'd trusted him, and why she still missed someone that she'd only met for the briefest of moments. Finally it had come to her. After spending her whole life training, punishing her body and preparing for being a Ranger, he'd been her first and her only friend.

Chapter 7

Joey

Having spent three days, three sleepless days, tracking Bracha from Murrayfield to the West-End of Edinburgh, Joey was exhausted. But hate pushed him onwards. Bracha hadn't slept in that time either; if he had, Joey would have found him by now. Travelling along the main routes, through Corstorphine and Haymarket, he'd made no attempt to hide his trail. It was plain arrogance on his part. Nothing else would explain his carelessness in taking such an obvious route or in leaving so many signs of his passing. He clearly thought that Joey wasn't a threat.

Reaching the inner fence-line at the junction of Lothian Road and Princes Street, Joey ignored the urge to push on and follow Bracha into the city-centre. Every cell in him screamed at him to go after Bracha, not just for Jock but to warn the women in The Gardens. They didn't exactly need his protection, nor would they welcome him from what he'd learned of them, but forewarning of a threat benefited anyone whether they welcomed it or not.

Finally he ignored the urge to pursue, to kill Bracha, and listened to the voice of Jock that had nagged him for to *be safe*, *make the smart choice; no heroics*. He returned to the small, fenced-off garden he'd spotted back at Coates Crescent. Sleep was a must, as was food if he was to be fresh enough to face the madman.

Edinburgh was littered with these gardens, surrounded by fences and often locked gates. They were assigned to residents or individuals who lived in the nearby townhouses. Jock and he had used these types of gardens often, finding that they were perfect for allowing them to relax. They could be confident that one of The Ringed wouldn't stumble across them in their sleep. They'd only had to worry about the living in these camps and they had plenty of improvised first-warning devices they'd designed for that task.

Jock. Grief slapped him hard across the face as he realised that he'd be setting up his first camp alone.

Deciding to do Jock proud, he stretched some light nylon rope between the boughs of two trees, draped a camouflaged tarp over it and pegged the edges into the soft mud with the metal spikes he had in his rucksack. He'd considered taking some of Jock's supplies – he had many items that they'd chosen not to duplicate – but had pushed the notion aside, opting to find new ones on the road rather than disrespect Jock by raking though his rucksack. Jock would have called him an eejit for his decision.

Spreading his second, smaller tarp on the ground, Joey busied himself with building a small fire. He could take the risk of The Ringed seeing the glow, as the fencing would halt their attempts to reach it. Dinner was a few leftover scraps of rabbit meat and some tomatoes he'd taken from a greenhouse in Corstorphine on his journey. Tomorrow, he'd pick up Bracha's trail.

Chapter 8

Alys

Alys had slept well and had finished packing her own things and Steph's, when a flash of movement outside the window caught her attention. Raising her eyes, expecting to see her cousin running around, she stiffened as she caught sight of a tall, oddly-dressed man standing a hundred yards or so from the girl playfully swinging a metal pole around.

Dropping her things and performing a quick check of her weapons in transit, she sprinted along the short corridor to the school's main doors. Halting for a single second to compose herself, she pushed the door open slowly in order to not startle the man. Alys kept her face relaxed.

"You must be Alys," the man said cheerfully and very politely. He had closed the distance between himself and Steph, who predictably had walked straight towards the stranger, curious about his unusual outfit.

Alys nodded.

"Stephanie, come here," she said.

"But Mr Bracha was about to tell me a story."

"Now," Alys said flatly.

Sighing loudly and making a big show of rolling her eyes and tutting, she stomped back to her cousin.

"Inside, and lock the door," Alys told her huffing cousin, watching the petulant youngster slam the door after her, but keeping her peripheral vision trained on Bracha.

"That wasn't very welcoming, young lady," he said, polite as ever, but allowing a little menace to creep into his tone.

"That's because you're not welcome here, Mr Bracha."

Smiling pleasantly at her, he interrupted.

"Oh, just Bracha, my dear. And, really, there's no need to be so rude. I'm just passing through. No harm intended."

dEaDINBURGH: Vantage • 105

Alys rested her right hand gently on the handle of the Sai on her right thigh. Indicating the direction he'd pointed with a jut of her chin, she replied, "Pass through then." Her mother's words coming from her mouth. This man, the way he dressed, moved and spoke, screamed out to her instincts that he was everything her mother had warned her men became in this city.

Abruptly he sat cross-legged on the road surface, resting his elbows on his knees. "Perhaps we could share a meal? I've been travelling for a few days without rest and I'm quite exhausted."

He examined Alys for a few moments, assessing her body, her face.

"No? Perhaps some information then? I'm thinking of introducing myself to a little community of women, along at Princes Street Gardens over there. Perhaps you know them?"

Alys clutched the handle of her Sai but did not unsheathe it.

"Ah, you do know them." Bracha beamed at her. "A whole community of women; fighters from what I've heard. I think that's worth a visit, don't you, Alys?"

Alys lifted her head slightly, assessing her options. He had no visible weapons, just the ridiculous-looking metal pole with the fat end he'd been swinging, but the lightness of his step and the flexibility he'd displayed in the smoothness of his movement and in sitting down all told her that he was a dangerous fighter. This was a man who knew how to use his tall, if slight, frame.

"You wouldn't be made very welcome there, Bracha."

Standing as quickly as he'd sat earlier, he spread his palms out to either side of his body.

"Oh, I'm simply wonderful with people. I make new friends wherever I go. Look how famously we're getting along, Alys."

He was trying to provoke her into doing something. She swallowed her anger and spoke in the same calm, flat tone she'd used throughout.

"Pass through."

Dropping all pretence at friendliness and levity, Bracha lowered his chin. Staring up at Alys, he took a few steps towards her, hands still spread, and smiled horribly.

"Or what?"

Alys gave him a humourless smile of her own.

"Or you don't get to pass through," she said softly

Bracha cocked his head to the side again, giving a sad looking expression, before speaking.

"Here's how I see this playing out," he began.

A fraction of a second later, Alys' Sai no longer sat resting on her right thigh but had instead travelled the short distance between her and Bracha and struck him dead centre in the forehead, knocking him clean out.

"Creep," she said to his blank face as she retrieved her Sai.

Darting inside, she pulled her rucksack on and helped her cousin into hers. Grabbing Steph by the left wrist, she yanked the girl towards the rear exit that led into the car park.

"I can't believe you did that, Alys. Why did you hit that poor man; you're worse than Aunt Jen."

Steph had pulled her arm free from Alys' grip and was glaring up at her elder cousin with contempt.

"He was only being friendly."

"We don't have time for this. Hurry up." Alys whirled around and headed for the exit. She'd taken three steps when she suddenly registered the sound of her cousin's footsteps running in the other direction.

"You idiot!" she yelled after Steph.

Racing after her younger cousin, Alys shouted for her to come back but the girl was tearing her way towards the front doors of the former school. Alys desperately yelled again for her to come back and then watched horrified as Bracha calmly stepped through the doors and slipped his arms around

Steph, who had run directly into his embrace like he was some kindly uncle.

Alys skidded to a halt and drew her weapons, dropping her rucksack as she moved.

"Mr Bracha, I'm so glad that you're all right," Steph beamed.

Bracha held her out at arm's length.

"Thank you, my sweet girl."

At that, he spun her around. Clutching the girl to himself, her back to his chest, he looped one arm over her shoulder. With the other hand he produced a stiletto dagger and pressed it to her right lower eyelid.

Steph looked in panic at her older cousin, realisation finally showing in her eyes.

"It'll be okay, Steph." Alys spoke to reassure the girl out of reflex. She needed to make sure that Steph didn't do anything stupid. That she followed Bracha's instructions.

"Your cousin is correct," Bracha soothed. "I won't do anything to hurt you. If you do what you're told." Bracha glared at Alys from behind Steph.

Dragging the girl along he backed himself out into the street, positioning his back to the sun so that the light made Alys squint to see him.

Silhouetted against the light at his back, he dropped all pretence.

"As I was saying earlier, Alys, here's how I see this playing out. Assuming you're willing to listen this time?" Bracha edged the point of his blade a half centimetre deeper into Steph's eyelid.

Alys re-sheathed her Sai and adopted a submissive open-palmed gesture, mimicking, mocking the one he'd offered her earlier.

"Okay. How old are you, Alys?" he asked.

The question took her aback.

"Eighteen," she replied, looking puzzled.

Bracha laughed loudly.

"Bloody eighteen-year-olds." He shook his head. "Then of course you were born here, Alys. You have no clue what the world was like before… this." He nodded his head to indicate the streets around them. "It was a horrible place, Alys, too many rules. Don't do this, don't say that. People got so uptight at the smallest little differences."

Alys wanted to yell or launch herself at him, but she had no choice but to stand and listen.

"Most people rushed around full of their own self-importance. They thought that they were invincible; that money, or an education, or status made them untouchable, infallible. Do you know what most people did when the plague came, when the dead rose, Alys?"

She shook her head.

"They tasted delicious. That's what they did. People like me; we were the ones who did what it took to survive. We adapted. We thrived in this world."

He laughed at his own insights.

"I'm willing to gamble that you know someone like me. Someone single-minded. Someone in charge. Someone who does what it takes to keep your community safe, to survive."

Alys felt her cheek twitch as his words hit home, closer than he might have suspected.

"Yes. You wouldn't be here otherwise, with your lovely Sai and your impressive skills."

"What do you want?" she asked.

"That depends." He paused for a second, clearly calculating or perhaps deciding something. "Have you heard that there's a cure?"

Alys narrowed her eyes, trying to work out if he was asking because he knew of one or thought that she did. She decided that, with Bracha's talent, honesty was best.

"No."

"Well I have" he beamed. "I learned that it's out at the Old Royal Infirmary. I learned this from a very reliable source."

Alys shrugged. "So? Go get it."

"Ah, that's where you come in. There are certain people in the south, beyond the inner fence-line, that I'm none too keen to see and who feel the same way about me. I need a little help. A half dozen or so of your fine fighting females would be just the right number. People who can do what needs done. That's what I need, survivors."

Alys shook her head. "They'd never help you."

"I think they will, you see, when I turn up at their gates with this one's head and you, broken and crying."

Alys controlled the urge to launch herself at him.

"They'll just kill you." She spat out the words.

"Hmm. Maybe you're right. Perhaps it would be better if I just held onto young Stephanie here as a hostage, whilst you lead me to The Gardens."

"Not going to happen," she told him, watching the tears boil from her cousin's eyes.

"You're not leaving me much choice here, Alys."

With a small flick of his wrist, he put the blade into Stephanie's right eye and flicked, causing it to pull free of the socket and dangle onto her right cheek.

Stephanie crumpled to the tarmac, taking Bracha with her.

Landing on his knees, Bracha propped up the unconscious girl, arm still curled around her. He moved his dagger to the other eye.

Alys had covered half the ground between them in the few seconds that had passed, but came to a full halt as she saw Bracha move towards her cousin's remaining eye.

"She's not going to die, Alys, but I'll take her other eye if you don't start being a little more pleasant."

Alys glared at the ridiculously lethal man.

"Okay, I'll take you there."

"How perfectly wonderful, Alys."

He smiled up at her from the road. "This one will just slow us down though."

Alys screamed as Bracha changed his grip on his dagger and plunged it at her cousin's chest. There wasn't enough time to reach him before the blade stabbed into her. Alys ran at him anyway. Drawing her Sai she tore along the road, watching his hand plunge towards the girl's heart in slow motion, knowing that she'd never make it.

"Aaaaargh!"

Bracha was suddenly screaming as an arrow tore through his right hand with such force that it threw him backwards, off Stephanie.

Never missing a step of her run, Alys flew at Bracha. She brought the Sai in her right hand down hard on his left wrist, breaking the radius and ulna instantly on impact. He shook off the pain instantly, impossibly, and began to rise to his feet, but she was already bringing her other Sai around in a backhand strike to the upper right arm. She heard the humerus break and brought her forehead crashing down on his nose. Alys would like to have spent a few more minutes breaking more of the monster's bones, but Steph needed her and Bracha was on his knees, arms useless.

As she threw him a final hate-filled glare, she became aware of the arrow in his right hand, just as another disturbed the air millimetres from her ear and tore across his right eye, leaving a mush of jelly and white gristle where his eye used to be.

Bracha climbed to his feet with the strength of insane rage and ran off down the street.

Turning to Steph, she kneeled and pulled her cousin close, not bothering to turn to look at the owner of the strong hand now placed on her shoulder.

"Let me see to her eye, Alys." His voice was much deeper than she remembered but it *felt* the same.

Suddenly exhausted, she sat on the road and watched him carefully and methodically clean

Steph's wound, remove the useless eye and gently bandage the empty socket. Stephanie, mercifully remained unconscious throughout. Alys looked at the back of Joey's hood which was still raised; she hadn't seen his face yet.

When he'd finished, he inspected the girl for a moment, brushed her hair over her ear with his finger and turned to Alys, lowering his hood as he did so.

"Hello Alys."

He smiled at her wearily.

Chapter 9

Joey

Alys punched him in the chest, knocking him onto his backside.

"Hey." Joey picked himself up. "Not much of a thank you."

"Don't leave it so late next time," Alys scolded him.

Just then, the girl with Alys who'd been injured began stirring and crying for her.

"Shh. I'm here, Steph," Alys told the girl, stooping to scoop her head up and cradle the kid.

"There's something wrong with my eye," Stephanie said. "I can't see. It hurts."

A fresh torrent of tears streamed from her one good eye.

Alys held her until the crying subsided.

"It's okay now, Steph. The man has gone and he won't be back in a hurry. Thanks to him." She gave a sharp nod in Joey's direction, noticing her cousin perk up at the sight of Joey's face.

Stepping forward, Joey offered the kid a hand, which she took, and he hoisted her up onto her feet. Alys stood alongside the younger girl, one arm around her little waist.

"This is Joey. He's my friend."

Stephanie raised her eyebrows as she looked at him, a puzzled expression on her face.

"You don't have any friends. Alys." Despite the tears and the pain, she laughed at her own joke.

Alys smiled sadly, and said simply, "Yes I do."

"We should get going, Alys. Bracha will be back," Joey said.

She raised an eyebrow doubtfully.

"After what we did to him? No way we'll see him again anytime soon."

"Yeah. I'd have said the same thing a week ago."

Joey spent the next few minutes explaining what had happened with Bracha a few days earlier: about Jock and about the satchel and its contents. Alys had surprised him by giving him an awkward hug, instead of punching him like she usually did. She'd looked genuinely shocked and saddened to hear that Bracha had killed Jock.

Within half an hour the three of them had collected their things, made a brief and successful scavenge of the Eye Pavilion building for sterile eye-patches and antibiotics for Steph and began the walk back towards The Gardens, Joey explaining how he'd tracked Bracha to St Thomas Aquin's.

"I considered stopping into The Gardens, well the fence-line at least, and warning your mother but my temper got the better of me and I went straight after him."

Alys smiled at the notion of him turning up at the gates of The Gardens alone. "Probably it's for the best that you followed Bracha, don't you think?" she said, glancing at Stephanie.

She turned her attention back to Joey. "Have you read any of Jock's journal yet?" she asked

He reddened a little and shook his head, subconsciously shifting his hand to Jock's satchel which was across his shoulder and resting on his hip. "No. I was a little preoccupied."

He should've just told her that he couldn't, but he knew that Alys could read and didn't want her view of him to be diminished.

Alys nodded. "What do you think that flash-thing is?"

Joey shrugged. "Dunno. Jock said I needed a computer to use it. Said it was my mum's. I figured that I'd just hang onto it and hope that I came across someone who has the means to use it while I'm travelling."

Joey suddenly came to a dead stop as he realised where he was. Standing at the junction of George IV Bridge and High Street, he touched a hand softly to the fence that formed the boundary of The Brotherhood's territory. It was the first time he'd been in the area since the night he'd scaled the fences with Jock and left The Brotherhood behind. These people had once been the only family he'd known and, regardless of their motivations, had given him a moral compass (of sorts), food and a safe home for fifteen years. A wave of shame passed over him as he realised that he hadn't thought once about his former home or the people he'd grown up with.

After a few minutes silence, Alys placed a hand on his shoulder.

"We should go. It's getting dark."

Joey still preferred the dark, or at least his eyes did, a throwback to his time in the underground crypts. Always, his most peaceful moments would come when he was in the absence of light. The darkness was a warm blanket around him and held no terrors. Recent experience had taught him that the monsters that walked in the daylight were to be feared more than imagined ones in the night.

As she made to scale the fence, Joey held her back. "I know a better way, easier." He nodded at Steph, who'd been walking silently beside them the whole way, holding onto Joey's hand.

Leading the girls through the ruins of the Bank of Scotland building, the three emerged on Lawnmarket and made their way quickly to the gates that separated The Gardens from The Royal Mile. Joey had pulled his hood up as they'd exited the bank, fearful that one of The Brotherhood would be on the surface. He couldn't know how they'd react to his presence, but suspected that the underground cult had changed little in their philosophy, outlook or daily routine in the years he'd been travelling the north with Jock.

Picking the gate's lock effortlessly, Joey slid through and then held back a little so that Alys could take the lead.

"Wise man," she said.

"Yeah. I figured that your face would be more welcome than mine."

Alys glanced at her cousin's bandaged face.

"Don't bet on it," she muttered, cutting a glance sideways at her cousin, before leading the three of them down the Playfair Steps towards her home.

Joey watched her go and smiled, despite the circumstances. It was good to see her. She looked good, *Hell, she looked great,* and really, who else did he have?

Interlude

Fraser Donnelly

"Jesus."

The man had been sitting at his post watching security footage from the dead city of Edinburgh for close to twelve hours. The pay was lousy, so were the hours, but he liked the solitude of his work. Being paid to monitor the CCTV network of the quarantined city was hardly demanding. More often than not he'd bring a bottle of vodka along on the night shifts and find entertainment in the lives of the abandoned.

His neck ached; it always did. His lanky frame wasn't built to lounge around in a chair for twelve hours a day, luxurious leather, orthopaedic or not. Leaning to the left and then to the right, a series of loud pops and cracks preceded a long groan of relief from him.

Standing, he pushed his hands behind him to his lower back and puffed his chest out as he pushed, feeling the muscles lose their tension as he watched the teenagers and the young girl make their way down the stairs towards Princes Street Gardens.

The boss would want to know about this. Pulling his seat towards him, he spoke into his Comm.

"Fraser Donnelly."

As he waited to be connected, he considered that although the extra money the Executive had been paying him these last few years for keeping a camera on this teenaged boy, Joseph, had been very handy, having to converse with Mr Donnelly, even by Comm, was never a pleasant experience. Still, the boy had crossed several zones since the old man's death, and Mr Donnelly paid him to relay this sort of information. Squeezing his butt cheeks he forced a loud fart out to relax, amusing himself with the notion that Mr D might be able to smell it through the Comm. He doubted that the man's facial expression would change in response, at any rate.

The face, neck and shoulders of Fraser Donnelly flickered into existence, forming a fully 3D holographic image on his desk top. Dressed in an expensive suit, appearance as groomed as always,

Donnelly looked coldly in his direction. He never looked angry or even annoyed exactly but his disapproval was a laser beam.

"What is it, Paterson?"

Aware that he'd been sitting staring slack-jawed for a few seconds, Paterson reported the day's events to his superior.

"Let me know if he leaves The Gardens. Other than that, don't contact me again."

Donnelly signed off abruptly.

Paterson relaxed into his seat and allowed a lazy and loud expulsion of gas to leave his backside, in retort. Reaching for the pack of Pringles to his right, he emptied a few into his open mouth.

"Once you pop you can't stop, Mr D," he laughed at his own fart joke.

Padre Jock's Journal

In the early days of the outbreak, people were so isolated, too isolated, or perhaps too innocent to realise that what was happening was the new reality for them. What they had, what remained in the city, this was it from now on. Twenty-somethings sat on their PS4s, thumbing away their worries or aggression on *Call of Duty* or *GTA*, comfortable in the knowledge that the screams and death they heard outside their barricaded doors were nothing to worry about, nothing that could affect them, and that the police or army, government or whoever would sort it out. Some of them only began to worry when their broadband was cut off; some of them when their Sky TV disappeared. When the electricity went off and all electronic devices died, that's when

Most people really started to get angry. When they couldn't Google or Tweet or whatever the hell those idiots did. And then the smart ones got scared.

Leaving their once-comfortable homes and stepping into the real world instead of the virtual one, reality hit them hard. Food, heat, the hungry dead and survival became their primary concerns instead of clicking *Like* on some picture of a cancer-ridden baby or a kitten with a grumpy face, or perhaps completing their new shoot'emup. Some rose to the challenge. They fought and survived, for a while at least. Most learned the difference between a virtual Zombie and a real-life one pretty bloody quickly. I remember passing by one guy, a hipster-type, dressed in tight trousers, check shirt, oversized hat and large-framed spectacles, frantically holding his smart-phone into the air, trying to get a signal as the dead devoured his legs. God only knows if he was calling for help or trying to update his Facebook status. *Being eaten by Zoms. It's different... LOL...*

Whatever he was doing, a few hours later he'd be dragging the upper body of his dead self around the old town looking for a meal; eyes glazed, fixed on

FRESH MEAT, HIS ONLY SOCIAL INTERACTION FOR ETERNITY.

Chapter 10

Alys

As Alys led Joey and her cousin along past the Scottish National Gallery, she kicked at a few discarded plastic burger containers that still blew up and down the terrace, left over from the German Christmas market that'd been visiting when the city had been hit by the plague. For someone who was generally of a stable, calm disposition, the last twelve hours had propelled her on an unexpected and uncharacteristic emotional rollercoaster. Bracha, Steph's injury, her rescue at Joey's hands, the boy with the bow suddenly coming back into her life, and now having to face her mother and her aunt with Steph injured, and *him* with her asking for shelter – the day had brought anger, annoyance, shame, fear, elation and then more fear. In the few short beats of the day, she'd been through a greater range of emotions than in the last eighteen years.

Glancing across at Joey, she watched as he supported her cousin on his back, chatting away to her about the people he'd met in the suburbs, making her laugh. How that was possible in the circumstances Alys couldn't fathom; she wouldn't have had the capacity. It wouldn't have occurred to her to try, but there Steph was, missing eye and all, laughing like she was on a day-trip to the beach. She wasn't sure that she liked it; how *easy* it was for him to be liked, to be free. Free with his emotions, and literally free, so very free in the world.

Steph's balance had presented as a problem the instant they'd begun their descent down the long and steep Playfair Stairs. Joey had picked the kid up on his back, calling it a piggy-back ride. Alys hadn't heard the expression before and saw little to do with pigs in the manoeuvre, but was again ambivalent in her reaction to Joey's solution. It was practical and Joey was impressive in his strength. He'd carried her the length of the stairs and was still wandering along with her on his back, not a care in the world, no sign of tiring, either of her or physically. She liked that. She'd always liked his strength and his character.

The ease with which the boy with the bow and her cousin had formed such a naturally comfortable relationship confused her. She'd always found it difficult, even with Steph, to display affection, to be physical with people unless she was fighting them. Joey and Steph played, walked hand in hand and just *liked* each other, she supposed, so easily. She sort of hated them both for their weakness.

The two sides of Joey had her angry at him, disgusted with and by him in truth, but engrossed in his movement, skill and capacity for survival in equal measures. She couldn't for the life of her figure out how this boy had survived so long beyond the inner fences.

As the thought crossed her mind, Joey, with lightning speed, dropped Steph gently to the ground, drew his bow, loaded an arrow and dropped to his right knee, aiming directly at her.

As she took a ready stance and began to draw her Sai, he let the arrow go before she even cleared leather with the Sai.

Alys heard a *thunk* behind her and rolled reflexively and tightly to her right, coming up on the balls of her feet, knees bent, facing the direction in which Joey had shot the arrow.

A Ringed, pretty fresh from the looks of it, was lying on its back with one of Joey's arrows sticking out of its forehead. Four more of the creatures were steps behind where it had stood. As Alys twisted the position of her feet, shifting her weight, and prepared to attack she heard four more *thwip* sounds followed by the same *thunk* she'd heard moments before. All four Ringed were silenced.

Joey walked past her, trying not to smirk, and began pulling his arrows from the downed creatures' skulls with a slurping noise coming with each removal.

In her state of over-alertness, she'd been totally oblivious to signs of the approaching creatures. It was so unlike her. Joey, whilst seeming relaxed, had been truly, totally alert.

"Smart-ass," Alys growled.

"You should trust me," Joey said, referring to her assumption that he'd been aiming at her.

"I don't even know you," she said, flatly.

"Yes you do, Alys," he replied giving her an almost one-fingered, almost rude gesture.

Despite herself, Alys laughed in response to his jabbing his middle half-finger at her.

"You should've gotten over that by now," she said, nodding at his part-finger. "I thought I was helping."

Steph rolled her eye at them.

Joey jabbed his half-finger at her again.

"Just trust me from now on."

She felt the smile leave her face; it felt so unnatural there and her facial muscles seemed to sigh as they returned her poker face to position. The laughter disappeared, carried off on the cold, cutting Edinburgh wind that constantly whistled along Princes Street.

"I will, Joey. I promise." She meant it completely.

Watching him pick Steph up again, Alys took the lead once more, taking them to the entrance to The Gardens. She felt Joey exhale loudly as they entered.

"It'll be okay," she told him, punching him sharply on the shoulder.

As he followed her through, Alys saw five women waiting for them just inside the entrance.

"It's me, Alys. Go and get my mother and my aunt. Steph's been hurt."

Some women Alys hadn't seen stepped out from the shadows. It was her mother, flanked by two of her guards. She hardly ever had her protectors with her. It wasn't a positive sign.

"Jade, Megan – take Stephanie to the medical tent and one of you go and get my sister," she barked at two of the group of women Alys had seen initially.

Jennifer stood staring at Alys, unmoving, unreadable. Finally Alys broke and took a step to her side. Using an open gesture, she indicated Joey with her hand.

"Mum, this is Joey, my… friend."

Joey took a step forward and then a ball-bearing to the forehead, delivered from the catapult of one of her mother's guards. Watching him crash to the grass, face first, she screamed at her mother.

"No! He's with me. He saved Steph… and probably me as well." She said the last part with shame in her voice, but she'd take the shame of being rescued by a male, if it meant keeping Joey safe.

Jennifer looked down at her daughter, crouching protectively over the boy with the bow. She was completely without emotion.

"No males. Ever," she said softly and left them on the ground together.

Chapter 11

Joey

Alys' mother threw a flurry of sharp punches, alternating between head and gut, gut and chest. Blocking each of them, he used her slight forward momentum against her, rolling her punch, extending the reach of it further than she'd intended. It caused her front foot to slide forward an inch, bringing her in to elbow strike range. It was a good move, she'd taught it to him, and she grunted her approval as she slid the foot forward as he'd predicted, but continued further than he had expected to sweep him off his feet and onto his rear-end with a crash as he lunged to make the elbow connect.

"Up, Boy." She'd already assumed her ready stance.

Joey gave her a lop-sided grin, mostly to annoy her.

"Nice move, Mrs Shep…." He almost saw the kick that connected with his chest that time. There was no doubt about it, he was getting faster. The training, her training, was paying off. He really had to stop antagonising her by referring to her as *Mrs* though.

"Up… Boy," she said once again.

She'd never once called him by his name in the three months he'd been allowed to stay in The Gardens. She spat out the word *Boy* like an insult. It *was* an insult in this place.

Rising to his full height, which was still a few inches short of Jennifer's, he gave her the smile again. *To hell with it,* he thought.

"Ready, Mrs Shephard." This time he managed to block and deflect twelve of her blows before he was knocked on his ass once again. He could swear that Jennifer broke a smile that time.

"We're done today, Boy. Go back to your quarters." She swished around and took off towards another training session with one of the younger children. *Good luck to them,* he thought.

"Thank you," he called after her. Normally she ignored his ritual thank you at the end of their sessions. This time, she paused, turned slightly and gave him the sharpest of nods before resuming her walk.

High praise indeed.

Joey plonked himself onto the frost-covered grass, sitting with his wrists resting on bent knees, and scanned The Gardens as his breath fogged the evening air. The greenhouses on the flat sections were busy with girls collecting tomatoes, peppers and other produce. He could see women working metal in the smith's tent, prepping meals in the kitchen tent, doing drills in the training rings and scribbling away in the school enclosure. The few boys who lived there – seven of them, each younger than he and sons of women who'd been pregnant or new mothers when the men *left* – were dragging hand-ploughs through a large section of field. None of them had spoken to him. They'd leave if he approached them. When he'd arrived, Joey had expected the boys to be pleased to see another male, but if anything they seemed frightened of him in a way that not even the youngest of the girls were. They simply went about their duties and acted as though he didn't exist.

Everyone in The Gardens had a role, a place in the structure. Everyone was important and equal; more or less. The women of The Gardens were a truly self-sufficient society, dependant on no one and nothing but their own hard work.

Joey climbed the slope up to the fence-line that divided The Gardens from Princes Street and scanned the long, once-busy centre of the city. Jock had described to him the city before the plague hit many times using words like 'beautiful', 'striking' and 'cosmopolitan'. When asked about the people, he'd often used the phrase, "streets full of busy fools." The streets were still full, but instead of teeming with workers, residents, tourists and shoppers rushing around, they were filled with an endless myriad of walking corpses in various states of decomposition.

It was a quiet evening, relatively speaking. The ever-present groan that vibrated dryly with the bottomless hunger that these creatures suffered, was a little more muted today. None of them bothered to take a swipe at him through the fence as he walked the perimeter, checking the fence's integrity. Those who noticed him at all merely followed him along with their dusty, frost-covered eyes as he moved. It wasn't apathy; they always got a little slower in the cold weather. As he made his way along the fence shaking rails, pulling on posts, Joey reflected on his time in The Gardens.

After Jennifer's initial refusal to allow him entry – not when he was conscious at any rate – Alys had been able to convince her mother to grant him access because of his help in treating and saving Stephanie. They'd had to agree that they would not spend any of their time together and that Joey must participate in their way of life fully. He'd spoken to

Alys only a handful of times since, the pair of them sneaking out into the surrounding streets to swap stories and share survival skills. Whilst Joey had the advantage in survival strategies due to his years in the north, Alys was by far the superior combatant. In the short spells they'd spent together they'd made good use of every moment, each absorbing knowledge and skills from the other.

He thought that she was currently out of The Gardens on a supply run in Stockbridge. Combat training, farming and security now filled his days. In addition to this, Alys had sold her mother on the benefits of having access to Joey's intel on the world outside The Gardens and the immediate area that the Rangers patrolled inside the inner fence.

Jennifer had sat with him for hours at a time, fascinated at what had happened to and was happening in areas of the city she'd known as a child or in the days before The Gardens was founded. Forefront in her questions was security. She wanted to know as much as he would relay about the people beyond The Garden's inner fence. That was easy; most of them, whilst damaged, were good people, trying to survive another day. There were exceptions, of course, the most notable being Bracha.

Jennifer had found it hard to believe that he and Jock hadn't had any prior encounters with the man. His actions in tracking them and killing Jock seemed entirely too motivated by personal reasons. Joey had just about convinced her that he was merely another wandering madman, albeit a hugely dangerous one.

Whenever they'd spoken about Bracha, an odd look had crossed her face. She'd asked many questions about the way he fought, how he'd conducted himself. The language he used. Jennifer never really explained what she had on her mind where Bracha was concerned, but had told Joey that from his descriptions she could tell that Bracha had been a soldier. "I was married to a soldier." It had slipped out in conversation but she'd noticed Joey's eyes light up at the prospect of information on Alys' father and immediately shut down, resuming questioning him on the city.

Jennifer didn't seem worried about Bracha turning up at the gates to The Gardens. And he had to admit, why should she be? No one person, no matter how clever, skilled or deranged, was a serious threat to the women of The Gardens. As for his assertion that a cure existed in the Royal Infirmary grounds, Jennifer treated the notion with the same ridicule that Jock had. Joey omitted Jock's warning of Somna and The Exalted. He didn't doubt Jock's account for a second, but how did you sell that tale to a stranger?

Joey, of course, had shown her the flash drive that Jock had kept for him. She'd described to him exactly what it did and explained that, without a working computer, there was simply no way to determine what its contents were. As she'd handed it back, an uncharacteristic softness entered her

dEaDINBURGH: Vantage • 141

features and tone, clearly sensing how disappointed he was in his inability to access the link to his mother.

"I'm sure you'll see what's on it one day, Boy." Her face hardened again as she handed him the device. "On your travels."

It had been a clear and none too subtle hint that it was time for him to move on. He couldn't help but agree. Having roamed the city for three years, he'd enjoyed his time in The Gardens, had picked up and passed on many useful skills and rested well. It was, however, time to go.

After completing his duties and chores under the ever-watchful eye of Jennifer's people, he slipped into the small tent they'd allowed him to claim during his stay. Only once in the three months he'd been here had he left the tent between lights-out and sun-up. As he'd become predictable, the night-time guards had been removed weeks before. Tonight would be the second time.

Slipping silently over the rails onto Princes Street, he looked over his shoulder, down at The Gardens to check that no one had seen him go. *All clear.*

Moving between the sluggish corpses on the main city thoroughfare proved simple enough with only a few of the more warmly-dressed ones reaching out to him or half-heartedly snapping their jaws shut when he passed. Taking Hanover Street, he headed downhill, along Dundas Street and down on to Brandon Terrace where he spotted the clock at the intersection Alys had told him to use as a marker. Turning onto Inverlieth Row, Joey spotted a faded maroon-coloured number 27 bus parked, two wheels up on the pavement. Inside, a warm glow flickered.

The area leading to the bus had been relatively free of Ringed but a couple shambled towards the bus, driven by the slope downwards as much as they were by the glow of the firelight. Joey sighed, drew his knives, Jock's knives, and silenced the pair before tapping gently on the vehicle's door.

Alys smiled through the fogged glass and pulled a lever to open the doors for him. The heat hit his face as he stepped onto the stairs to board.

"Any problems getting out?" Alys asked, shoving the lever in the opposite direction as soon as he was inside.

"None."

Looking around the bus, Joey noted the fire in the space where disabled passengers once parked their wheelchairs. Jock had taught him what the little blue and white sign had meant in the old world. The disabled had been amongst the first to fall to the plague, for obvious reasons. In his entire life, Joey had met only one person in a wheelchair – a lady by the name of Suzanne Dalgliesh. At least that had been her name in the Old Edinburgh. Here in the dead city, she went by the name of Suzy Wheels.

Suzy Wheels occupied a bungalow on Groathill Avenue; she had since before the plague. With its modified ramps, access points and lack of stairs for shuffling feet at the ends of dead legs to climb, Suzy's home should have been one of the first to be invaded. Anyone who'd ever met Suzy Wheels did not need to ask why that didn't happen. A former Tai Kwando Olympian, Suzanne had been in a traumatic accident two years prior to the plague and wrecked her spine as well as her car.

She'd fought her way through eighteen painful months of physiotherapy and another six months in the gym, sculpting her upper body, building the functional muscle she needed and perfecting the technique required to fight from her chair. That had been her goal: enter the next Olympics, Rio 2016 – "The Olympics, mind, not the Paralympics," she'd say – and kick asses from a seated position. Joey could fight, but he had no doubt at all that the sixty-year-old *invalid* could kick his ass all day long from the comfort of her modified wheelchair.

Taking a seat across from Alys, who had resumed her place at the other side of the little fire, Joey picked out a potato that had been baking in the flames and began eating it.

"So what's up, Alys? Couldn't we have just passed notes, same as always?"

Alys shook her head. She'd sent him a note asking him to meet at the bus via another Ranger and Stephanie. The other Rangers were slightly afraid of her and passed on her messages without asking any questions. Joey could relate.

"We needed time. A few notes passed slowly over weeks just isn't good enough this time," she replied.

"Okay," Joey said through a mouthful of potato. "What's the story then?"

Alys shifted her eyes to the fire.

"I want to go to the Royal Infirmary. I want to go after the cure, Joey. I want... I need you to help me."

Joey took his time chewing his food, giving himself a chance to work out what to say to her. He needed an answer that wouldn't earn him a burst lip.

"Alys." He tossed the potato skin on the fire and began staring at the same spot in the flames she'd picked. "There is no cure. Jock said so. He's been there."

Alys continued to stare into the fire.

"To the hospital? He's searched it?"

"No," Joey conceded. "He hasn't searched it, but he was confident that the cure was just a story made up to bring people to the area."

Alys looked at him now, confusion and hurt showing in her eyes as the flames danced across her pupils.

"Jock told me that there's a group of men, dangerous men. He called them The Exalted, and they live nearby. He said that they're killers on a massive scale, that they use stories of a plague cure to lure people in. Some of the things he told me about these guys were pretty grim, Alys. I never once saw Jock frightened of anything until he told me about The Exalted and their leader, Somna. He only told me to warn me to keep away."

"Did he tell you where they are? Exactly where they are?" Alys asked.

It wasn't the response he'd hoped for but there was no point in lying to Alys.

"Yes."

Pulling a map from his rucksack, he began drawing lines around Drum Woods, The Royal Infirmary and Liberton, telling her everything that Jock had told him of the people and the area.

Alys sat back, leaning against the back of a passenger seat.

"There's plenty of scope to get in, do a search for a few days and get out unnoticed, Joey."

It was hard to argue, but he did anyway.

"If you'd seen Jock describe that place," he pointed at Drum Wood, "and those people you wouldn't want to go."

Something slid over Alys' face, changing her expression from that of his friend to the one that her mother wore. "I'm going and I'd like you to come, but I'll go alone if I have to," she said flatly.

"Why, Alys?"

She was on her feet standing over him in an instant, pulling him up by his jacket lapels. "You have to ask? The chance of a cure, Joey? Why wouldn't we go?"

Joey didn't resist her as she pulled at him, but brought his face close to hers until their noses almost touched. It was a dirty tactic – she hated intimacy – but it was the only way to make her back off a little. Anger or any physical confrontation would only earn him a new scar.

Pulling in until he felt her breath on his cheek, he told her, "There's nothing there. Why are you so convinced that there is?"

Instead of moving away, she surprised him by staying close and bringing her hands up to his cheeks. Holding his face, she made him look into her damp eyes.

"Because of Bracha. He believed it. He believed it so much that he was trying to raise a group of fighters so that he could get in and out. He was scared of Somna's men too; maybe even Somna himself. He believed it enough to face the monsters Jock was so frightened of."

Joey took her wrists and pulled her hands away from his face. She allowed him to.

"Bracha is a lunatic. You're taking a risk like this on the say so of the murderer who tried to kill your cousin?" Joey choked back a wave of emotion. "Who killed Jock?"

The coldness crept back into her face and her voice.

"I know what he did, Joey. Maybe we'll get a chance to repay him. He'll be headed the same direction, to the hospital, only I think that he wants to destroy it. I think that he loves the city the way that it is, and that he'll find that cure, if it exists, and he'll make sure no one ever benefits from it."

Joey's muscles had stiffened at the thought of getting close to Bracha again. He could feel that she'd noticed the shift in him. She knew that he had begun to consider the idea and she pushed a little harder.

"We simply have to go, Joey. For The Brotherhood, for The Garden community, for Jock." It was her turn to play dirty. Joey flinched at his mentor's name.

"We could be free, really properly free."

A single tear had broken loose and rolled down Alys' face. She truly believed the words she'd said to him. He ran through several weak justifications in his mind, the most pitiful being that it would be for Jock, this trip. It wasn't: Jock would beg him not to go.

In his heart, he knew that she'd given him the only reason he needed to agree to go. She was his friend, his only friend, and she needed his help.

"Okay," he told her. "But we plan first. We do it my way. In and out. No heroics."

Jock's words coming from his mouth.

"Agreed?"

Alys tossed him a smile that reached her eyes for a change and punched his arm to seal the deal.

"Agreed."

Chapter 12

Alys

A sudden push against the bus sent it wobbling to one side. Alys and Joey both snatched their weapons up and stood to look through the misted windows.

"Didn't you have a check around before you arrived?" she snapped at Joey, more out of shock than genuine anger.

"Of course I did," he said calmly.

Both turned their eyes back to the window. Alys stepped forward to rub some of the condensation away with the sleeve of her coat. She gasped as she looked out onto Canonmills. Joey pressed his cheek against hers to get a better look through the gap she'd made and let out a little sound of his own.

The bus was surrounded by The Ringed. Every panel, front, side and rear, was being pushed upon by a herd of them, three deep in parts. Each of them was completely fixed on the bus, lips drawn back from snapping teeth.

"Where the hell did they come from?" Joey asked. "You ever see that many in one place?"

Alys shook her head.

"You?"

Not like that," he replied. "They're all pretty fresh.

By fresh he meant fast, vicious, dangerous and, of course, hungry.

There was little chance of them pushing the bus over; they simply didn't have the strength or coordination for that, unless they got lucky. The greatest risk to them was that the hands that had begun to slap against the windows would eventually break the glass. Neither of them was particularly worried about a Ringed climbing through a broken window – they were too high for that – but that smashed glass would definitely mean exposure to the bitter winter wind howling louder than the groans of the dead outside.

"Upstairs," Alys told him, leading the way to the top deck.

From the top they gained a better view of what they faced. Alys guessed maybe sixty Ringed, all fresh, had surrounded the bus. She rubbed her temples thinking, *What the hell brought so many of them here?*

Canonmills was outside the inner fence, but only just, and so generally was fairly clear of the dead. Those she had encountered recently in the area had been older ones, slow and part-frozen with the winter frost.

Glancing along the aisle of the bus towards Joey, who had his face pressed against the rear window, she gave him a sharp whistle. When he turned, she pointed up at the ceiling, eliciting a conspirational grin from him, followed by a quick nod of approval.

Stepping on Joey's interlocked hands, she boosted herself up towards the skylight, pushed it open and climbed through, out onto the snow-covered roof, before dangling her arm through to help Joey up.

"I'm cool," he told her. As Alys withdrew her arm, Joey's hands grabbed the skylight and his feet suddenly shot through, followed by the rest of him, head last. He landed lightly on his feet in a crouch.

"Show off." She shook her head at him. "Let's see what we've got."

She headed towards the edge to lean over. Her sudden presence above brought a surge of hungry groans from below.

"You think you can shoot them off? Maybe just clear a section for us to break through?"

Joey had a quick peek over.

"Na. Too few arrows, too many heads to shoot. How about we go back to the lower deck and just start braining them through the windows after they've broken through?"

Alys scowled. "Too risky. Too easy to get grabbed or bitten whilst reaching out."

Joey's face suddenly broke into a wide grin. Hooking his bow over his back, he went through his ritual of checking his weapons, tightening his laces and pulling his hood up, before cocking an eyebrow at her and flashing an even wider grin.

"Back in a minute, Alys," he laughed and leaped from the roof onto the nearby bus shelter, from where he did a tight sideways somersault, landing on top of a phone box several feet away. With a final cartwheel-tuck, he spun off the phone box, landing catlike on two feet behind the row of The Ringed, who still faced the bus.

Launching into a song, he took off up the hill towards a burnt-out Esso petrol station, sixty-odd dead shuffling behind him like a grotesque parade.

"Searching for answers and finding more reasons, not to believe in the bullshit they feed us…" Joey sang loudly and out of tune, laughing as he ran and tumbled and spun his way up the hill away from the bus.

He's entirely too full of himself, that boy, Alys thought, supressing a smile.

Returning a few minutes later, Joey had doubled back around The Ringed who were still headed up towards Rodney Street. Joey was walking towards her, arms wide in a *what d'you think* gesture. Alys shook her head.

"Nice singing, Joey."

He laughed loudly. "You like that? Jock taught me it."

He launched into another verse, ducking as she launched a right-hander at him.

"Shut up, idiot. You'll have them back down here." She nodded up at the herd of Ringed. Some of the rear ones had lurched around and were looking in their direction, teeth bared.

"Okay. Let's go tell your mother that we're running away to find a cure at The Royal Infirmary, which is, by the way, surrounded by murdering madmen who worship a Zommed-out footballer. That'll be fun."

Alys cocked an eyebrow at him. Deadpan she said, "Okay."

Padre Jock's Journal

I almost knocked Father Grayson on his ass today. Having returned from cleaning up some twenty-odd Ringed from the fence-line along at North Bridge, I was exhausted and in no mood for any of his usual closed-minded decrees. Unfortunately I had to seek permission for something. Good God, having to ask anyone's permission grates at me but doing so of this... man, Jeezus help me.

He argued with me for an hour but finally caved in when I asked him, *Who'll guard your borders when I'm too old, or dead?* Father Grayson scowled at me like never before, but eventually promised that you wouldn't be put forward for Communion, that I could train you in a few years, and more importantly, you would be allowed to keep the bow I'd acquired for you and the freedom to train with it.

I never wanted this for you, Joseph, living in these dungeons, worshipping the dead. You're too clever, have too much spirit for a life in The Brotherhood. Sometimes I pass you in the corridor and you look just like one of them with your head down and face passive. It makes me sorry that I brought you here and wish that I was a better man. A man who could be a father to you. I learned from my own kids that that's not who I am. It's better that you're brought up here.

Other times I watch you from a distance, when you think no one is around, up on the surface. I like that you show this small defiance to them. I promise we'll leave this place one day, but only when you're ready, only when you won't die outside these fences. For now, the bow is yours and I've ensured that nobody will take it from you.

Chapter 13

Joey

Pulling the bow string back to his nose, Joey let out a gentle breath and loosed the arrow. Another shot. Sighing, he ran along towards the traffic lights in which his arrow was embedded, executing a half-hearted somersault over a rusted traffic island as he went. Alys was very late and his bones had stiffened in the cold waiting for her outside the old Scotsman Hotel on North Bridge. Alys' departure from The Gardens must have proven more difficult than she'd anticipated.

Joey had departed The Gardens a week earlier, thanking the women for his time there and for teaching him so many useful skills. Jennifer, stoic as ever, had simply told him "Goodbye, Boy." He'd been tempted to give her a hug, *just because*, but hadn't fancied nursing a facial wound for the next few days.

Saying goodbye to Stephanie had been a much more difficult experience. In his time in The Gardens, Joey had become very attached to the girl, who had taken to following him around whilst he performed his duties. Alys thought her behaviour the result of a crush on Joey, but it wasn't that at all. She just wanted a big brother. In a way, she'd transferred her need for a male role model onto him, and he was quite happy with that. It was nice to have someone who simply liked him for being him.

What Alys felt towards him was a mystery. What were they to each other? Allies? Potential lovers? That didn't feel right. He did have feelings for Alys – he loved her he supposed – but how did one know what love felt like? Best friends felt like the most comfortable fit for them. What he did know for sure was that he wouldn't be asking Alys about it anytime soon. They had a job to do.

Steph was quieter than she'd been previously, according to her mother. She was more circumspect and spent long hours deep in thought watching Joey or the trainee Rangers go through their paces with Jennifer and her team. In the evenings, they'd sit together, she and Joey and her mother, sharing stories and laughing together. Steph and her mum were so easy to be happy around in stark contrast to many of the others in The Gardens. Spending time in their company made him feel part of a family for the first time. Gradually Steph withdrew from these nightly visits.

As the weeks passed, she'd retreated into herself a little more. With each passing day she spent more and more time alone. Gradually her self-imposed exile passed, but the Steph who emerged was quite different from the carefree kid she'd been only weeks before. She enrolled in her Aunt Jennifer's Ranger programme. Initially refusing her niece, Jennifer had conceded to grant her admittance after Steph had turned up every day for a month, stationed herself right at the heart of the class and punished her soft body, copying the much more experienced trainees' drills and exercises. Eventually, Joey had asked why being a Ranger was suddenly so important to her. "I won't ever be a victim again, Joey," she'd replied.

On the day he'd left, Steph had refused to speak to him and stood alone in the training field practicing combat drills and sequences as he left by the north gate.

Alys, on the other hand, was coming with him, or rather, he was going with her. She was still adamant that Bracha would be going to the Royal Infirmary in search of the cure. And she was still convinced that they had to stop him. She dangled the chance to repay Bracha for Jock's murder in front of Joey. He had to admit, Jock's death was still a raw scab inside him, and if he allowed himself, the urge to kill Bracha could consume him.

Jock had taught him better than that. He'd taught him to survive. Bracha would get his, sooner or later. Men and women like him always did. It didn't matter whether or not Joey was there to see it. Still, if the opportunity arose, he wouldn't waste it either.

Alys was due to return from her current Ranger tour a few days after he'd departed. The plan was that Joey would use seven days before meeting Alys on North Bridge to gather any supplies, clothing and tools they might need from the outdoor stores along Rose Street. Taking an indirect route along Clerk Street, they'd leave the inner-fenced area and then loop around Craigmillar to the hospital grounds. Their journey, of only four miles, should take around ten hours, what with the debris, cars and any Ringed they'd have to deal with or avoid along the way. Once they left the relative security of the inner fences, the Ringed population would likely be much, much denser as most of the land they would be travelling through was once residential.

They'd scheduled two days for the trip, to give them the opportunity to explore the area a little, and packed accordingly. Slow, steady progress was their intention. Stealth was more important than speed.

Most of the mountaineering shops had been emptied over the thirty years or so since the plague hit, but people had taken mostly the larger items – sleeping bags and such like. The smaller equipment, certain types of clothing and camping gear still lay in some of the stockrooms.

Whilst Joey scavenged for supplies, Alys would be speaking to her mother about her intention to leave the safety of the inner fence, travel south and look for the cure. As angry as Jennifer would certainly be, she respected her daughter's abilities and her judgement. Alys would be here, sooner or later.

An hour later, Alys appeared, dressed for the weather and carrying an empty rucksack and a sour expression on her face.

"Your mum a pain in the ass?" he asked.

Dropping to one knee, she began stuffing the supplies that Joey had left in a neat pile for her into her rucksack.

"Let's not talk about it, okay?" she said without looking up.

"How's Stephanie?" Joey asked.

"She… determined."

Joey jerked his chin up in a *how'd you mean* gesture.

Alys stuffed the last of her things into the rucksack and sat on top of it to look up at Joey.

"She's still training really hard, working on compensating for the eye. She's taken up archery."

Joey's eyebrows popped up, partly in surprise and partly in delight.

"Made her own takedown recurve bow," Alys continued. "Did you teach her that?"

"No. Not how to make the bow, or how to shoot one. She watched me make a bow though, and spent hours watching me shoot."

"Crush."

Joey blushed, more out of annoyance than embarrassment.

"It's not a crush, Alys. She just needs something safe to focus on."

Alys looked unconvinced.

"She any good?" Joey asked.

"She's *very* good."

Joey nodded. Steph had, knowingly or not, chosen the one weapon that her missing eye would actually give her an advantage with.

"So. We ready then?"

"Yeah." Alys nodded over to the line of cars running the length of the Bridges and onto Nicholson Street. "Over the roofs?"

Joey grinned. "You up for it?"

"Yep."

"Let's go then." Joey tightened his rucksack, laces and checked that his weapons were secure. The ritual was a comfort to him. He heard Jock's voice in his head reminding him of the precaution each time

With a small hop, he placed one foot onto the bumper, then the trunk, then the roof of a rusted Honda Cr-V. Running along, slowly at first to gauge the grip of his all-weather hiking boots on the icy car, he found the rusted car body underneath the layer of snow and ice gave more than enough traction. He increased his pace, leaping from roof to bonnet to trunk to roof, throwing in the odd spin or whirl when the space allowed. Running along the line of rotting shells of cars was by far the easiest and fastest route along the rubble, debris and vehicle-strewn streets.

After clearing his tenth vehicle, Joey spun around on the roof of a Mini Copper to check on Alys' progress. She was only two cars behind. Since the herd of Ringed at the bus in Canonmills, Alys had found a new appreciation for Joey's method of moving through the city. "It's so fluid, so fast," she'd told him. Alys had asked him to show her the basics the very next day.

Like everything else Alys Shephard had put her mind to, she punished herself practicing the routines and manoeuvres associated with Parkour that Joey taught to her. Fortunately she had three things in her favour which allowed her to progress quickly. Firstly, she had been practicing gymnastics and unarmed combat for most of her life. The necessary strength, flexibility and basic balance were already at her disposal. Secondly, she was highly motivated. She hated being less able than anyone at anything. Finally, she was a total natural. She was beautiful and flowing in her movement across, over and through the city's surfaces and objects.

Nodding at her, she gave him a signal to carry on. Joey smiled to himself, happy to share his world as they flowed along the cold metal. After an hour or so, they reached the corner of the inner fence where Clerk Street met Hope Park Terrace. They found a gap that someone else had made in the chicken wire fence and re-tied with copper wire, presumably after passing through.

"Bracha?" Alys asked, pointing at the scar on the fence.

"Could be anyone, Alys."

Alys sniffed at him in reply, pushing her way past him to untangle the wire, reopening the hole.

"Ready?" she asked, nodding over at the group of the dead who were congregated in front of a Sainsbury's store. Some of the creatures had turned towards them in response to the rattling of the fence.

"Let's do it," Joey said, stepping through after Alys.

Taking a sharp right, they took a pre-planned detour they'd discussed when planning the trip. The Hospital for Sick Children was barely half a mile from their position, and whilst in the heart of a packed residential area, student residences mostly, both agreed that it would be a good place to scavenge some supplies. Neither expected it to take them quite as long as it did to reach their destination.

Almost every step of their path to the children's hospital brought another Ringed to them. Walking corpses in a myriad of varying states of decomposition barred their path in staggered waves, making them fight for every forward advance. Joey stood back and loosed arrow after arrow into the heads of the freshest-looking corpses as Alys whirled around, a flurry of Sai strikes, fists, feet, elbows and knees, dealing with the slowest ones sequentially. She was quite something to watch.

Clean, fast strikes, clinically delivered with no fuss, no energy wasted, no quarter needed. She scythed her way through the dead, stepping from one to the next as they fell behind her. It looked like a choreographed dance from Joey's viewpoint, making the violence she engaged in strangely beautiful and totally terrifying. For every one of The Ringed that Joey's arrows found, she silenced three. It was a devastating display of her abilities and one that showed Joey how easy she'd taken it on him in their sparring sessions. The disclosure of how much she'd been holding back for him startled Joey.

They fought and silenced former people of all description. Doctors, soldiers, students and children. An awful lot of children and teenagers. They sent them all to a peaceful existence, one in which they were no longer driven to wander the bitter streets of Scotland's former capital for eternity trying to sate a bottomless hunger. That's what they told themselves, anyway. They had to believe that the people they silenced were at last *truly* dead or the actions that they took would be meaningless. Closure for poor wandering souls trapped in rotting corpses was all they had to offer and all they had to cling to. Even though they called them The Ringed and occasionally Zoms, neither of them ever forgot that they used to be people. In his mind, Joey still clung to the phrase *The Children of Elisha*, but in his deeds he did not.

Slowly but steadily, they made their way along Sciennes Road through a tide of the dead to the gates of the hospital. Both were glad of the hours they'd spent conditioning their bodies for sustained combat, but the training they'd endured couldn't compare in intensity to the real-life gauntlet they'd run. Both were exhausted when they reached their destination. Both hid their exhaustion from the other.

"Some fun, eh?" Joey asked, retrieving an arrow from the eye socket of a Zom dressed in a tattered, weather-beaten nurse's uniform.

Alys slipped her Sai into the sheaths on her thighs. Ignoring his question, she nodded in the direction of the hospital's gates.

The stone pillars and walls of the gates still stood but the metal of the gates had either been torn down or had rotted. To close the gaps where the gates once stood, someone had parked four large food trucks across the entrance and packed sandbags around the space between ground and truck. It wouldn't hold against the living, who could just move some sandbags and slip under, but it'd keep the dead from entering the hospital grounds just fine. Joey suspected that whoever was holed up inside the hospital probably didn't have many visitors with a pulse. The horde of Zoms they'd dealt with to get there would deter most travellers.

No heroics. The phrase struck him suddenly. Jock would have been pretty angry at what he'd just done to get to a hospital that had probably been looted decades before.

"I'll go first," he told Alys. She always resented it when he took point, but swallowed her reflexive need to lead, simply because he had the long range weapon. Pushing a few sandbags aside, they both slipped through the gap. Joey was in a ready position in a second once they reached the inner line, scanning around for signs of people, dead or alive, whilst Alys replaced the sandbags behind them.

"Clear," he called.

Alys drew her Sai. Moving into point, she led him up the stairs and through the broken glass entrance. The sound of groaning faded behind them.

Chapter 14

Alys

ONCE INSIDE, ALYS SHIFTED HER SAI so that the handles rested firmly in her palms and her index fingers lay along the hilts. She wanted the extra reach as the corridors ahead had several twists and turns. Pausing to read the faded lettering on a map of the hospital, she opted to take a left turn towards the main building when a flicker of movement caught her eye on the right. Pointing her right Sai in the direction, she indicated to Joey to go slowly and quietly.

Hugging the corridor's walls, they moved along, slipping silently along the dark corridor, Joey with blades in hand and bow tucked away, watching their rear. They were wary but not particularly afraid. The Ringed didn't do stealth; their groans were involuntary and the smell of decay that emanated from them warned of their presence more often than not.

Alys stopped suddenly as a shadow slid across the gap at the bottom of the double doors she'd been moving towards. The shadow moved quickly, smoothly and with purpose. That meant a living person. Joey was facing the other direction so she lashed out a quick, gentle kick to his heel to signal that he should stop. She peered through the darkness at the gap under the door. Silently swapping positions she gestured to Joey that he should look through the gap. His night vision was far better than her own.

"There are two people there; small, fast," he whispered to her.

She tugged on his sleeve and made a circular motion with her index finger, indicating that they should swap positions once more. When back in point, Alys slid silently up to the door and held up three fingers to Joey behind her, slowly retracting them one at a time in a countdown.

They crashed through the double doors, weapons raised. Two children, no older than ten, dropped a pile of plates they'd been carrying, screamed and ran. The smashing of the plates echoed along the corridor long after their screams disappeared into the ward up ahead.

"Your face did that," Joey said.

"That scowl of yours would scare the dead."

Alys threw a few colourful phrases his way and hid a smile.

"Let's go say hello," she said, following the kids along the corridor.

Taking an L-shaped corridor along to Ward One, they walked deliberately and slowly, weapons sheathed but accessible.

"Hello there," Alys called along the corridor. "We're sorry for scaring you. We won't hurt you."

They heard shuffling from deep at the rear of the ward.

"We just want to talk to you, maybe have a look for some medicines in the hospital and then we'll leave. Is that okay?" Alys said gently.

"Let's just go." Joey tugged at her shoulder.

Shrugging him off, she told him, "No, Joey, they're just kids. They might need our help."

She saw his eyelids flicker and knew what he was thinking. She cut him off before he could say it.

"No heroics, I know. But if not us, then who? Who'll help them?"

She could see the surprise cross his face, just for a second, before he hid it. *Why were they all so surprised when she showed that she cared? Her mother was the same, but Jennifer's expression was always more one of disdain. Did they think she was made for violence and nothing else?*

"They might not need any help, Alys. They seemed fine."

She turned away from him. "We're going to make sure, okay." It wasn't a question.

Alys moved through the doorway onto the ward, ready to call again, when a young and shaky voice called out.

"What age are you?"

"We're both eighteen," Alys answered instantly.

Whispering came from behind some curtains at the rear.

"You're adults," a different voice said, an older one, a girl.

Alys smiled at Joey who had a *what the hell* look on his face.

"Yes we are. Almost, but not quite, I suppose," she said with a hint of humour.

"Are you hungry?" called the second voice.

"I'm starving," shouted Joey. "I could eat a scabby dog."

Alys punched him in the arm, the usual spot.

"You'll scare them."

"You eat dogs?" a third voice asked, an even younger one this time.

Alys glared at Joey to keep his mouth shut.

"Why? Have you got one for me? Is it a Jack Russell? I love a nice barbecued terrier, so I do."

The youngest kid cried, "Nooooo. Don't eat ma dug," and appeared from behind the curtain, looking crushed.

Fifteen older children stepped out, laughing at Joey's remark.

The oldest-looking one, maybe sixteen or so, bent down to bring herself face to face with a three-year-old who was clutching a stuffed dog to her chest.

"He was only joking, Natalie. He won't eat Dougal."

Turning to Alys, she held her hand out. "I'm Irene" she said with a sad smile. "Sorry, but we're a little wary of adults around here... Since they all tried to eat us."

The group of kids all snapped their attention towards Alys, looking like they half expected her to suddenly decide that she did fancy biting one of them after all.

"You think that all of the adults became…"

"Biters," Irene interrupted. "All of them. They got them out, the kids who were here in the beginning, on bite-night. At least that's what we were taught."

"Only kids allowed," little Natalie piped up.

Alys smiled at the little girl with the stuffed dog and back to Irene again. They thought that the plague only affected adults.

Alys felt Joey's surprise and resented him for it as she knelt down in front of the timid three-year-old, took one of her hands and kissed the back of it.

"See? I'm nice and warm and I'm only nearly an adult. You're safe with me, sweetheart. I wouldn't hurt you for anything."

Little Natalie insisted on taking Alys for a tour around the section of the hospital that the kids inhabited. So she wandered off with her and a group of the younger kids, leaving Joey with the teenagers.

 She was surprised to discover that the little group of children, thirty in total, actually had a pretty decent standard of living. The hospital still had running water and even had a functioning hot water system, heated by solar panels on the roof. The water was recycled rainwater and wasn't likely to run dry any time soon. Perhaps most surprising was that the kids – they called themselves The Sick Kids – had access to limited electricity which they used mainly for special treats, like watching old discs they called DVDs on little televisions built into the ward walls.

Alys had never seen a television before, and despite Joey's best attempts at an explanation, she was no more enlightened. Of course his explanation was second-hand from Jock. Joey had never seen a live screen before either. Neither of them had ever had any access to electricity.

The kids explained to her that the television never received a signal and neither did any radios they had. The only contact they had with the outside world was when the older kids went on supply runs. Generally they stayed within a small radius, but had been forced to venture further recently, leading to a horde of Zombies following them back home a week or two ago. Alys explained that the horde outside wouldn't be a problem in future and suggested some new ways that they could use to sneak around for supplies more discreetly.

Despite their confinement and ingrained distrust of adults, The Sick Kids were very open about their lives and seemed happy. They wanted for little, despite looking very pale and sun-deprived to Alys eyes. She thought that she saw signs of rickets in a few of them and made a metal note to suggest that they use the gardens surrounding the hospital more frequently to soak up whatever sun Edinburgh had to offer. The grounds were secure enough for that.

On returning to Ward One, Alys found Joey surrounded by most of the kids, animatedly telling stories about some of the people he'd met on his travels with Jock. The younger kids laughed until they were in tears, doubled over at his description of a guy he'd met who thought a panda was his wife. The teenagers were playing it cool, but she could tell that they'd been laughing too and would be repeating the tale to each other later in the day. Several of the older girls played with their hair and blushed every time Joey looked in their direction. All were amazed at his description of Jock as an old man, clearly astounded that he hadn't turned.

As the evening wore on, they asked The Sick Kids about the possibility of finding some medicine or other medical supplies in the building. The kids explained that they did have some supplies but had none to spare, insisting that they'd exhausted whatever stocks had been in the hospital to fill their own store.

Irene turned out to be as nearly a good a storyteller as Joey. As the oldest she was in the odd position of being in charge, but also being next in line to have to leave according to the rules that The Sick Kids Lived by. She gave them the thirty-year history of The Sick Kids, guilelessly. Alys sensed that a lot of what had been passed down through each shortened generation had been lost or altered to the point where no one really knew anymore how they came to be the community they were.

As Irene told it, the kids who'd established the boundaries and claimed the hospital as their own had been patients who'd been forced to fight for their lives against the very adults who'd been treating their illnesses just hours before. Irene explained to them that a small group of around fifteen had survived the initial outbreak. Witnessing mainly adults running around trying to eat kids, they assumed that adults were the only hosts and systematically cleared the hospital of all infected. Any kids who'd been bitten were either silenced or, more often, pushed out onto Sciennes Road. The founding kids essentially barricaded themselves in a little community, shunning all adults. They called them *biters*, but allowed other kids to enter the hospital once they'd been checked for bites.

Once a Sick Kid's eighteenth birthday came, within a few days they willingly left to save their family and friends from what they expected to turn into. When asked what became of the people who left and wandered out into the world without supplies, food, water, or any real survival skills, the kids looked puzzled and replied, "They just do what all the other biters do, they don't need those things."

Alys had asked, "What if they don't turn? What then?"

"Every adult becomes a biter," Natalie had said. The certainty of the *fact* made something break a little inside Alys. She didn't reply. What could she say? They lived in an insular little world where kids got older and were banished. The kids who remained were either descended from the original group of children or were kids whom they'd encountered on supply runs.

Deciding to stay the night at the younger kids' insistence, Joey and Alys made a little bed each for themselves in a single unit that had once been used to isolate chest infection patients. As Joey lay on the camp bed and Alys sat up reading by candle light in the rusted hospital bed, squeaking the rubber under-sheet every time she moved. Joey giggled, assuming that she'd farted. Alys hid her tears for The Sick Kids behind the book she read.

When she'd composed herself and was certain her voice would be steady, she spoke.

"What do you make of all this – these kids and how they live?"

Turning to his side to face her, Joey propped himself up on one arm, exposing his archer's chest a little. Alys' eyes were instantly rigid on one word on page eighty-seven of her book.

Joey thought nothing of being shirtless in front of anyone. Back in The Gardens, he'd habitually peeled off his upper clothes whilst training with her mother. Alys didn't think that she'd ever get used to seeing boys' bodies.

"I reckon that they're coping pretty well. If you think about it, it's a pretty logical assumption that they've made: that all the adults are monsters," Joey whispered.

"Oh I know, it's just that they seem to be in denial about it. They can look out their windows anytime and see children… Zoms who were children, right outside their windows. But they still ask their oldest to leave."

"I'm not sure we have the right to interfere, Alys. People don't like having their beliefs challenged," Joey said, sitting up.

Alys fixed her eyes even more rigidly on the page in front of her as Joey's sheet slipped to his waist. She forced boredom into her reddening expression.

"I think I need to do something, Joey. They're doing well, but they need older people."

"Why?" he asked, genuinely puzzled. "They've managed fine for decades with just a group of kids."

Alys did look up now, fixing his eyes with hers.

"What about those kids they turn out? They *are* still kids at eighteen here, Joseph; they're so naïve and they're being sacrificed out of fear and misunderstanding."

Tears had begun to burn behind her eyes. She willed them not to flow.

Joey nodded. "We can't just tell them that everything they've based their community on is wrong. Even if they accept it, the guilt will destroy them."

Alys rose from her bed. Sitting on the edge of Joey's camp bed she avoided looking at his torso or into his eyes and picked a spot on the floor. She reached out for his hand.

"Joseph. I really need you to help me with this. I need to find a way to make a small but significant change for these kids. Can you do that for me?"

Joey looked away. He was angry but hiding it from her. He was too alert not to notice that she'd called him *Joseph* twice now and too smart to misinterpret the use of the name as innocent. He knew that she was trying to manipulate him and he knew that she'd done it with the full knowledge that he'd recognise the attempt.

The gamble was that calling him Joseph would touch him somewhere inside, remind him of the man who was a father to him. The only person who'd ever called him Joseph, not Brother Joseph, but just Joseph.

Alys was gambling that the shift in his emotions would remind him what being a trapped kid was like. She'd been trapped by fences and her mother's insistence that she be ready to venture out. He'd been trapped by religious beliefs and loyalty to those who'd raised him. She wanted to remind him who he'd been to her and to Jock, but most of all to himself.

"Okay," he said, voice tinged with regret and a trace of anger. "Let's talk it through, but Alys," Joey clenched his jaw and gave her a hard look, "don't pull this crap with me again. Friends don't do that."

"I'm sorry, Joey." They both relaxed a little as the name left her lips. "I promise, I won't."

Chapter 15

Joey

THE HOSPITAL CAMP BED had proved surprisingly comfortable. Certainly Joey had spent the night sleeping on worse. He and Alys had managed a full four hours sleep after spending the early hours discussing how best they could help The Sick Kids. Still unconvinced that they had any right to burst the children's little bubble and open their eyes to a larger world, Joey trusted that Alys was seeing something that he wasn't in the situation. Despite being good with people, especially kids, he hadn't exactly spent much time around children and she seemed so certain of the need to change their viewpoint. Joey was having a hard time understanding how the *real* world that they were about to open these kids' eyes to was, in any way, an improvement over the one that they existed in right now. Affecting enthusiasm for her plan he ploughed on, despite the inner voice telling him to leave them to their fantasy.

Pulling on his black long-sleeved T as Alys read her book, Joey asked, "Ready?"

Alys snapped her book closed and stuffed it into her rucksack. Standing, she made for the door in reply. As she approached the exit, she turned towards him, a softness in her eyes he'd never seen there before.

"This is the right thing, Joey. I promise."

He gave her a sharp nod and followed her out and along the corridor to the former PJs' loft, a parent's room in the hospital where exhausted parents unwilling to leave their sick child could grab a few hours restless sleep. That was before they began eating their kids, of course.

The Sick Kids were spread around on the floor, resting on cushions and stuffing their faces with meat. Joey had no idea what animal it had come from and didn't ask, choosing instead to throw his rucksack into the corner and sit beside some of the younger kids and stuff his own mouth, signalling to Alys that she'd be doing the talking this morning.

Alys scowled at him, dumped her own rucksack at her feet and took a deep breath, composing herself. Her voice filled the room.

"Kids," she said, softly but firmly. It was a tone of voice Joey hadn't thought her capable of. She was always so… hard. It reminded him of the shock he'd felt when Alys had been so kind to Natalie the previous day. He thought that he'd hidden his surprise but Alys had clearly been hurt at it.

"Kids. We have to move on today but we wanted to tell you how impressed we've been with the way that you've organised yourselves here. You're strong people, with a good strategy for surviving this city. Better than most, as you've learned from Joey's stories."

A few of them giggled as Joey made a silly face.

Alys was clearly giving him a cue to say something. He smiled behind a chunk of meat and shoved it in his mouth, giving Alys the thumbs-up to continue. She drilled him with a look that would scare a Zom before turning back, smiling, to her audience.

"We're both really grateful to you for sharing your home with us." She glanced at Joey again; another thumbs-up. He tried really hard not to smile.

"Before we carry on with our trip, we wanted to tell you some more about the world out there." Alys pointed out the window. "Not all adults are Zombies. It's a fact. It obviously seemed that way because of the circumstances your predecessors founded your community in. But it's simply not true, I'm sorry."

Irene stood, dropping her meal at her feet. She had a sympathetic look on her face, like she was talking to a complete moron. Joey watched Alys' anger flash for a moment in response, but she buried it quickly before any of the kids noticed.

"Our founders knew what they were doing, Alys. Look out the window." It was she who pointed this time. "They're all adults out there; we're all kids in here. It's pretty obvious." She threw Alys another look of sympathy. "I know that it must be difficult to accept, but in a few months, maybe weeks, you'll be one of them."

Alys massaged her temple before speaking.

"Irene, I know adults who are still human. I've lived with them my whole life. I come from a community filled with them. My own mother's one of them. So did Joey. He told you about Jock, weren't you listening?"

Irene looked down at the kids gathered around the room. All were looking up at her for answers. She smiled kindly down at them, shaking her head slightly, communicating to them silently that Alys was clearly a nutcase.

"Joey told us about Jock, yes, but maybe he was an exception. Maybe he hadn't been exposed, or maybe…" She turned a malicious look towards Alys, eyes steely. "Maybe, he's a liar and you are too. Maybe you feel the turn coming on you and want to make sure that you've plenty of food around for you."

Irene made a gesture with her hands, a spreading motion like she was sowing seeds that took in every child in the hall. In a way, she was sowing seeds and ones that would grow quickly and wildly in her young charges' minds.

Alys backed up a few steps and crouched down to come to eye level with the kids on the floor, addressing them instead of Irene.

"Nobody is going to change. Nobody is going to hurt you, least of all me or Joey. We'd rather die first than hurt one of you."

Her voice conveyed passion, determination and complete conviction to everyone's ears. Everyone's except Irene's. She tutted loudly.

Joey did speak now.

"Alys is right," he boomed with a depth in his voice he'd never summoned before. A couple of the younger kids jumped in response. "We would never do anything to hurt you."

He stood, offered his hand to Alys who accepted and allowed him to help her to her feet. Standing together, facing the assembled kids, Joey continued.

"That includes staying in a place where children are afraid of us." Joey was suddenly as certain as Alys was that The Sick Kids needed a wake-up call. Bringing his mouth close to Alys' ear, he whispered, "Tell them everything, Alys."

She squeezed his hand firmly in response. *A thank you for accepting her judgement?*

Her eyes, filled with certainty and compassion, fixed on Irene's for a second before scanning each of The Sick Kids' faces in turn.

"The only thing that makes people turn into biters is being bitten by one. That's it. Not dying: if you die, you don't come back. Nothing else but being bitten will infect you. Not being spat at or breathing air around a biter or reaching eighteen years old."

Joey gave her hand a squeeze to reassure her to go on. They'd discussed this as a last ditch effort if The Kids wouldn't listen. Joey hadn't been convinced last night but Irene's single-mindedness and her influence over the smaller children reminded him of his life with The Brotherhood and he was damn well convinced of the only right course of action now.

"The people you've sent out there," Alys continued, allowing her anger and frustration to show, "these children you've sent out there in fear and ignorance and guilt have most likely turned by now, but only because you sent them out there to get bitten. You sent them out there needlessly, to die."

There it was: the truth of it. Alys moved her eyes over every face gathered, looking for a response.

Irene wasn't the least bit affected by their words. Gathering the kids together, she spoke sweetly to them like some bastard version of Mary Poppins, reassuring them, herding them.

"Come along kids, say goodbye to Alys and Joey. They're leaving now. That's it, come along."

Joey and Alys watched the children file out of the loft. All were smiling happily, some skipped as they went. The awful truth was that, for them, whatever Irene said was true; just simply true. No question.

As Irene passed them, indifferent to their presence, Alys' hand lashed out and caught her wrist in her iron grip.

"You're deluded." She spat the words at Irene.

Irene just shrugged, looked at her wrist until Alys sighed and released her. Then she floated off down the hallway singing to the children.

Alys glared at Joey.

"Don't," she warned. "Don't say a word."

Joey had no intention of saying the words but he was thinking them.

Not "I told you so," which is what she'd expected, but rather, "You were right to try."

She didn't want to hear either remark so he swallowed the words and followed her out onto Sciennes Road to continue their journey south.

As they made their way back onto the main thoroughfare of Dalkeith Road, Alys, who'd been silent since leaving The Sick Kids, turned to Joey.

"You think that they'll make it."

"They have so far, Alys." Maybe not the way that they could have but at least they're surviving."

Alys started along Dalkeith Road. "But at what cost? Are they monsters, Joey?"

"No," he replied instantly. "They're not. Maybe the younger kids listened. Maybe your words will sink in as time passes and they see evidence of it as they age. Maybe not."

Alys sighed heavily. It sounded like she was releasing something that had shaken loose inside her.

"Let's push on, all the way to the hospital today, Joey. Even if we need to travel all night."

Joey merely nodded in response. A sharp nod that told her he understood the urge. He'd felt the disillusionment that she'd been hammered by this morning during his travels with Jock. The realisation that some people couldn't, wouldn't be helped. It was a hard lesson and a difficult fact to accept. It was the driving force behind Jock's mantra of *No heroics.* She was handling it much better than he had.

They set off, south along Dalkeith Road, along roofs and trunks and bonnets. Car to car they flowed, much more quickly than they had the previous day, much more silently.

Chapter 16

Alys

They reached Craigmillar Castle road by midnight and silently set up camp on an overgrown cycle path set slightly off the main road. The sprawling trees and shrubs left just enough moss-covered path to erect their tents, but provided enough in the way of obstacles to snag any wandering Ringed. Between the foliage and Joey's early-warning devices they could rest easy. At least Joey could; Alys' brain was on fire.

She was furious and devastated at the day's events. Joey fell asleep the instant his head rested, leaving Alys in awe at his skill in emptying his mind. She ignored the urge to throw an arm over the boy who lay peacefully dreaming beside her, rolled over and spent most of the night grinding her molars.

Chapter 17

Alys

Morning broke and brought the smells of cooking meat drifting through the open doorway of the small tent. Reaching out with her right hand, Alys verified that Joey was up and about and no longer in the tent. She sat up in her sleeping bag and stretched the kinks from her neck.

Despite her mind's best efforts at torturing her the previous night, Alys had fallen into a deep and peaceful sleep. The moss-covered former cycle path had been the most comfortable surface she'd slept on for a week or so, more so than even the hospital bed. As a result she was feeling alert and positive. The campsite was mostly silent; the only sounds breaking the silence were the crackle of fat spitting as it dropped into a fire and the ubiquitous groaning of the dead. Alys didn't even register the latter. It had been the soundtrack to her life. She only paid attention to those sounds when they became desperate or aggressive or were close by; not the throbbing, passive need, the torture of eternal hunger that the undead felt and expressed habitually.

Leaving the relative warmth of the tent, which smelled strongly of Joey as well as the roasting meat, she stepped out into the frosty morning air to find two rabbits, suspended above a small but very fierce fire, rotating on a hand-cranked rotisserie. Joey's bow and quiver rested against the trunk of a sycamore.

"Morning, Alys." He smiled at her.

"Hey, Joey."

"Feeling better about yesterday?" he asked.

Alys sat cross-legged on top of a little camping mat he'd laid out for her.

"Yeah. I still think we should check up on them, in a few months. Maybe just look in on them without letting them know that we're there?"

Joey made a little gesture, indicating that he was fine with that.

He did that kind of thing a lot – made movements with his eyes, body or hands, instead of speaking. It wasn't something she'd been used to in The Gardens, but a boy who'd lived in silent darkness for most of his life was bound to have a few odd mannerisms. When he did speak, he didn't waste words. His softly-delivered statements always had purpose and he never spent them on idle chit-chat.

"Thanks, Joey," she said. Alys would go anyway, with or without him, but she'd much rather they went together. The realisation of this need made her harden her voice a little.

"So, you've been busy this morning." She jabbed a thumb towards the rotating bunnies and then another at his bow. "You use the bow?"

He gave her another nod. Choosing not to speak once again, he indicated that she should choose a rabbit for breakfast.

"Wait there for a minute." She darted off into the wooded area around the cycle path.

She scanned around the shrubbery, stepping between thorns and brambles, selecting an array of brightly-coloured berries, flowers, tubers and some unappetising-looking leaves, before returning to the fire.

Removing the rabbits from their spinning stick, she picked them clean of meat, throwing the pieces into a food can along with water, leaves, flowers and some of the tubers, which she'd broken into chunks.

"Give it half an hour," she told him, placing the can into the ashes at the side of the fire to simmer.

Alys handed him a handful of blackberries and raspberries.

"These'll keep you going for now."

Joey moved his nose over to the can and sniffed at the steam rising from it.

"What's in it?"

"You never used local plants when you were out travelling the north with Jock?"

Joey shook his head. "We just ate meat most of the time; never any shortage of that. I did miss the potatoes and onions The Gardens would bring up to The Brotherhood, though."

Alys prickled at the reminder, but hid it from him.

She pointed into the pot. "That's spinach, or close enough that we can call it that."

Shifting her finger around she pointed out green beans, mint, parsnip and carrot, none of which Joey recognised.

"There's good energy in the vegetables and the other leaves will make the meat taste better."

She watched Joey take another deep sniff of the steam.

"Smells amazing, Alys."

"Yeah, well, are you going to sit there smelling your food all morning, or are you ready to discuss how we should approach the hospital?"

Joey's smile disappeared.

"You think that Bracha is already there, don't you?"

Alys nodded.

"I do. And not just because of the cut fence back there. He's desperate to find this cure, Joey. He wanted help, but I reckon that he's realised that he's not going to get it and has opted for stealth instead of force."

"I've no problem hunting that… that man," Joey said. "It's just that after what I… we did to him last time, he'll be ready for us, Alys. This guy's a monster, more so than any of those things."

Joey jerked his head in the direction of some of The Ringed who were tangled in brambles at the end of the pathway.

Alys hadn't met many males. Aside from Jock (barely), Joey and of course Bracha, she'd encountered maybe twenty of them on her Ranger patrols; a few of whom she'd spoken to, and some of whom she'd been forced to kill. Despite her lack of exposure to them, one thing that seemed common to all of them was that they misunderstood and completely underestimated women.

Alys had been raised to believe that all men were weak and not to be trusted. She'd been taught that The Gardens were safer, better-defended without that weakness present. Whilst she hadn't entirely bought into the notion, she had allowed those beliefs to shape her, to build her in body and soul into a lethally clever, immensely skilled and very dangerous woman. A Ranger.

Every single one of the men she'd encountered had failed to see that. They'd been blind to the resourceful and determined woman who stood before them and had attempted to protect, molest, intimidate, control or ignore her in their exchanges. Alys pitied them and despised them in equal measures.

And Joey was sitting here, trying to protect her from Bracha despite all he knew of her and her people, despite the history they shared, the connection and the provisions the strong women of The Gardens had given The Brotherhood who raised him. Despite the training he'd received from Jennifer. It was a cold, hard slap across her face and a startling reminder of her mother's words, drummed into her since infancy. "They're weak; they'll try to control you. Pity them, but don't trust them. Ever." Alys was so disappointed in the boy with the bow.

"You really think that you need to tell *me* that?" she asked, stone-faced, voice filled with contempt. "After what happened to Stephanie? I looked at that man for three seconds and knew everything about him, Joey. I knew how he moved in combat from the steps he took. I saw how lethal he was from the way his hands spoke for him; every gesture betrayed the deadliness of those hands. I saw the predator in his posture, in his eyes. Just like I see the warmth, the concern in yours."

It wasn't a compliment.

Alys stared hard at him, baring her teeth enough that she had to speak through them. Perhaps to keep the anger that raged through her from exploding onto Joey.

"I see everything, Joey. I see how patronising you are and how weak your concern for me makes you. I've trained my whole life. You know what I can do in a fight, but you sit there telling me that I should be careful, like you're better equipped than me or more able."

She lowered her voice, made it much more threatening.

"Don't ever think that I need you Joey. You're so… arrogant. Soft. You don't face your anger or your desire to make that man pay for what he did for Jock. You with your stupid rules, your checks, your mantra. *No heroics.*" She spat the phrase out. "You haven't even had the guts to read that man's journal. Who the hell did you think he wrote it for?" Alys glared at him for a second and hurled a final insult. "Jock would be ashamed of you. Coward."

His eyes filled with moisture, making her all the more convinced at how useless he was to her, despite his skills. He really was weak. Jennifer was right. She always was. It was time to ditch Joey and deal with Bracha on her own. Find the cure and be the hero that this clown was too weak to be.

Alys stood. Turning back to the tent, she grabbed her possessions and began stuffing them furiously into her rucksack. She became aware that Joey was now standing, glaring at her through the tears that boiled down his own face, tracing clean tracks through the soot that covered it.

"I can't read it." He wasn't sad, despite the tears. He wasn't angry and he wasn't upset or hurt. He wasn't any of the things that his tears suggested. "I can't read at all." He wasn't hurt, no. He was embarrassed. "I'm not scared *of* you, Alys, and I'm not scared *for* you either." He placed a shaking hand on the satchel that held Jock's journal. "I was taught that survival was the most important thing. Not revenge. I want to kill that man so badly, but Jock wouldn't want that." Joey's whole body shook with anger now. He was barely holding it back.

Alys decide to push him a little harder.

"Jock is dead." It was brutal honesty at its best, or worst? But he needed to move on from the guilt and obligations to his surrogate father that he carried around like a dead weight. "Bracha will be back for you, or for me. Bracha might already have this cure, if it exists. Our survival is utterly dependent on removing this bastard from the face of the planet. Jock would tell you to kill him."

Suddenly Joseph MacLeod broke inside, right in front of her. His shoulders sagged, his eyes lost the fire of anger they'd possessed moments before and his legs lost their strength, dropping him to his knees onto the moss.

Voice a whisper, he wept harder.

"Jock told me that man had to die. He said we should kill Bracha the first day that we met him. I talked him out of it."

Alys walked towards him and placed a hand on his shoulder. He wasn't weak at all; he was, in fact, a very strong man who hadn't yet taken the time to grieve for the only parent he'd ever known.

A memory of her own father itched at her, making her wince. Escaping from a long-forgotten cell in her subconscious, an image leapt across her mind's eye. The man with the calloused hands, brown eyes and wide smile bounced her on his knee. She must've been four and was squealing in delight. He sang 'Mary had a Little Lamb' to her, whilst her mother scowled at him. She mentally shoved it back into the darkness.

"Would you like to read Jock's journal with me? All of it?"

"Yes," he said, with everything in him. "There's nothing I'd like more."

Chapter 18

Stephanie

Feet side-on to her target, left arm solid but supple and holding her bow loosely from her body, Stephanie drew back the bow string smoothly, touching it to the tip of her nose, not to her cheek as her instructor continuously asked her to. She simply didn't care what the archery teacher had to say. She'd seen Joey use this method and Joey was the best. So far. She was determined to be better.

Her arms ached, having lifted and strained and pulled for over four hours, repeatedly loosing arrows at the target Joey had used during his time in The Gardens. He'd told her that when he fired an arrow, he visualised it hitting the target and then just *made* it do so. She'd been trying to do the same for weeks but Joey's visualisation technique hadn't worked for her until she began to see every target as Bracha's left eye. Then she began to pile every arrow, one after the other, into the exact spot she wished them to go.

She had the bow, perfectly made after fifteen attempts, from old plastic pipes and twine. She had the will and the technique and the motivation. Now she just needed to change herself, to build a body that wouldn't betray her aim. That meant hundreds of hours of shooting. That required her to focus on combat and archery, nothing else. Not her friends, not her mother and not how much she was already missing Joey and her cousin.

She had a long way to go, but had an endless engine of hate to propel her there. Any time she tired, she'd picture *his* face, touch her patch-covered eye socket and resume her exercises.

Patience, she told herself with every draw of her bow. *Patience*, she told the jackhammer in her chest that threatened to explode from her body in white-hot rage each time she thought of Bracha. *Patience; be ready; be ready for him. You'll get your chance.*

With her back to the Castle, she loosed another perfect shot that travelled forty feet across The Gardens and struck the centre of a hay target that looked to her exactly like Bracha's face whilst a group of kids her age watched her.

Patience.

Chapter 19

Joey

Joey raked through the shrubbery searching for the plants Alys had found for them that morning. He wanted to duplicate the meal she'd so easily put together for them, but this time with some venison from the deer he'd killed an hour before. Alys was back at their camp cleaning the animal. The fur, meat, some of the organs and a few of the long bones would all come in handy at some point. The meat most of all could be wrapped in cling film that Joey had in his rucksack and would keep for a few days, maybe a week, in the current temperature. Most likely it wouldn't even require cooking before consumption until day three or four.

Having initially planned to travel to the hospital, less than a mile along Craigmillar Castle Road, they'd had a change of heart after the morning's events and had spent most of the daylight hours devouring Jock's journal. Alys had patiently helped Joey through each page, assisting him in reading the contents. Waiting until he stumbled over a phrase, she'd softly correct him or finish a word rather than just read the whole thing for him. "You need to learn, and fast," Alys had said several times as he'd complained about his ineptitude, offering her the book to read for him.

He wasn't anywhere near so bad at deciphering the words as he'd expected to be. Jock had begun to teach him to read, but their practice sessions had been spent looking at street names on maps and on buildings they'd passed. The street names were always so clear, in black, printed capitals. Jock's journal, filled with looping, swooping and curled letters held only confusion, embarrassment and fear for him. At least initially.

As he'd been forced by Alys to try to read through the hand-written text, he became aware that his perception of the individual letters and words was slowly improving. Initially he'd had to mentally convert stylised letters into their more capitalised equivalent. As he made his way through, page by page, this process became quicker and was beginning to feel instantaneous. Alys, despite how demanding she generally was, turned out to be a patient teacher. Whilst he doubted that he would be able to decipher every word on his own, yet, with her help, he was making quick progress through the journal.

Both he and Alys devoured the pages. Jock's journal disclosed answers to questions they'd been asking their whole lives. Questions nobody seemed to want to give answers to and brushed off with "What difference does it make now?" in reply.

The book was filled with explanations of how the plague broke and how the city became sealed, and information about the world that had existed before the plague as well as the people who'd lived then and how they'd lived. It was simply the most exciting account of the history of their city they could have hoped for. They read of Jock's family and his struggle to keep them alive. His own survival, the bouts of despair and depression he fought through. Joey's mother's horrific death, in more detail than either of them needed. They couldn't and wouldn't stop reading, though, until it was complete.

As the journal progressed, it became obvious that Jock had spent the last years of his life dedicated to watching over Joey and eventually to teaching him everything he needed to survive the dead city. He'd begun writing the journal in his time with The Brotherhood and it was clear that what lay inside the pages was meant for Joey's eyes alone. He'd loved Joey as deeply as he'd loved his own children and had been determined to see him become a strong man.

Joey and Alys laughed and cried and raged and struggled through every word of the journal until it was done and the day had disappeared around them. They'd sat in stunned silence for maybe an hour afterwards before chatting over a few of the more shocking aspects of Jock's account. The secrets they found inside, the revelations, and the discovery of them together brought them closer than they imagined possible.

The outbreak. The speed at which the city was abandoned. How horribly over-privileged and self-absorbed, how pampered and arrogant the people of Jock's former world seemed to them. It was a shock to both of them. How easy the people of the early twenty-first century had life and how little they seemed to actually live those lives. They seemed so trapped – truly caged, not by fences but by the limitations they put on their own lives, by the things that they valued and the things that they didn't. Their world seemed so dead to Joey and Alys.

The new insights horrified them and saddened them. It made them hate the people of the past. It also made them glad, for perhaps the first time, to be born into a place where people actually lived instead of just existing. In a city of the dead their parents had built the first living, thriving, proactive and capable communities the country had seen in generations. It gave them both a strange sense of pride.

They looked over at the nearby dead with fresh perspective. Still groaning their dry groans, snagged on foliage all around. Shuffling blindly through their new existence, focused on a goal that would never satisfy them. One group of Zoms, furthest from their camp, were gathered around the steaming corpse of a badger they'd brought down. Three of them tore chunks from the twitching animal's flesh as their fellow dead watched Joey and Alys. Dozens of pairs of dusty eyes and hands followed the pair as they moved around the camp. Due to his upbringing, Joey had always felt pity for the dead and never more so than now.

They spent ten minutes folding away what little there was of their camp, saying nothing. The silence was a comfort to him. Along with the darkness it made him feel at peace, able to think. He and Alys had breached some of the walls that had stood between them and he felt more strongly than he had ever done for her. What those feelings were, he still didn't know, but she was pretty much all he had left now that Jock was gone. He had no intention of losing her.

Alys grabbed at his left sleeve as he made his routine checks of his equipment.

"You hear that?" she asked.

Joey craned his neck to the side and signalled to her to stay silent. He rotated his head as he listened all around. They'd agreed to risk travelling at night because the number of Zoms who'd been drawn to their camp throughout the day had reached a level where the possibility of them breaching the tangle of shrubbery and trees into their camp, by sheer weight of numbers, was becoming a probability.

Scanning around, he signalled again to Alys to extinguish the burning torch she carried. Joey's eyes had begun to adjust to the creeping darkness but he wanted the light completely gone so that they could reach their peak.

Standing still for several minutes, listening, watching, he noticed Alys crouch beside him. She was more silent in a crouched position.

Joey's ears and eyes did their work, piercing the darkness, seeking out the smallest movement. Snapping of twigs, dry, dusty groans that grew louder, clumsy footsteps. He counted, and counted, and counted. *Five, twenty, forty.*

Eventually the sounds became less distinct and formed a din rising all around them. The dead were hungry. They'd sensed a meal and had gathered in number. Joey's best guess was that there were well over three hundred walking corpses, obscured behind the twisted and moss-covered trees and shrubs that lined the one-time cycle path. They leaned against the natural barrier; a unit, pressing, pushing, and reaching.

Alys tugged at his trouser leg.

"How many?" she mouthed.

He watched her jaw stiffen as he mouthed a reply.

She nodded and stood, bringing her mouth close to his ear to whisper.

"We've no choice, Joey. We have to run."

The heat from her breath in his ear brought goose bumps to his skin that even the realisation of being surrounded by the dead hadn't provoked.

He turned his head to whisper into her ear.

"Let's wait until one breaks through."

He pointed at a swaying, creaking section to their left.

"Once they break that section, they'll funnel through it together. They always follow each other, right? We should be okay if we keep ahead and run towards the hospital."

Alys shook her head. "They're just as likely to break through several sections at a time. Besides, they'll keep following after us unless we give them something else to chase. They don't tire, remember? We do."

"Just go for it, then?"

Alys gave him a sharp nod and sprinted off along the cycle path. Despite the danger, Joey grinned broadly at her receding back before pushing off after her.

Almost immediately the foliage to their left began to collapse and the dead poured through. As Alys had predicted, section after section broke, releasing Zoms in varied states of readiness and decomposition into their path, ahead and behind them. Most were old, dried and badly decayed, but some were fresher, dead maybe a year at most. Almost all were dressed in the tell-tale uniforms and pyjamas of hospital staff and patients.

A quick exchange between them communicated that the thinnest group lay ahead. Joey drew his blades, one in each hand, and turned on The Ringed to their rear whilst Alys and her Sai ploughed through three Ringed like they were made of paper.

Joe silenced five, one after the other, with kicks, blows from the handle of his right blade and the edge of his left blade. One of those he kicked, a man in a shredded business suit with his throat torn wide open, picked himself up from where Joey had knocked him to the path, still very much in the mood for a snack. He chomped down onto Joey's right foot, dislocating his jaw as he slid his mouth around the toes. Joey's right hand flashed down, driving his blade through the back of the creature's head as he felt pain shoot through his foot and up his leg. He kicked the Ringed off him and stamped the back of its head in a rage of fear. *It bit me!*

Joey whirled around and saw Alys, ten Ringed at her feet and a clear path ahead, staring at him with wide eyes, filled with shock.

"Move," she yelled at him as another large group burst clumsily through the treeline behind him.

They ran hard, punching, kicking and stabbing a path through the seemingly never-ending stream of Ringed, crashing like a flood onto the path behind them, in front of them, beside them. Adrenaline drove them and allowed Joey to ignore the pain in his foot and the fear in his heart. He had one thought: *get Alys out of this before I turn.*

Suddenly the narrow, tree-lined path filled with the hungry dead opened out into a wooded area. Joey and Alys shot out from the narrow path into the open space, taking formation in the centre of the clearing, back to back. The wood was filled with the dead also.

They were surrounded, front, centre and rear. Hundreds poured along the cycle path in a raging torrent of hunger and death to join hundreds more of their undead brethren already shambling their way along. Joey and Alys took their stances and began fighting.

Wave after wave of green splintered teeth, broken-fingered hands, foul-smelling feet grasped and clawed for them. Alys had pulled her sharpened Sai and was spinning it along with her standard one, severing hands, puncturing skulls and breaking faces. Most of the former hospital residents and staff were in the final stages of decay, meaning that bone and structure disintegrated easily under the lightest blows. The fresher ones were getting closer, though.

When they reached the pair at the centre, the fight would be a different beast.

Joey hadn't bothered pulling out his bow. He felt sick, dizzy and weak. *The bite?* Besides, The Ringed were far too close. He continued stabbing, clubbing, tearing and silencing the dead, making his shoulders ache and his legs tremble.

Tirelessly the dead shambled towards them. Relentless in the eternal hunger, they crawled and tripped and shuffled over their fallen comrades. The fresh ones, faster, more powerful and more resilient, finally reached the centre.

Joey stole a glance at Alys. She was a lethal whirlwind of death with a hundred Ringed in pieces and at peace at her feet. She had never looked fiercer, calmer. She'd never looked more beautiful. But even Alys couldn't keep this pace forever. She wasn't tiring yet, but it was in the post and he himself was only standing out of sheer bloody-mindedness. He hit another Zom and glanced back at her. She seemed to be working herself a little room, an exit route he hoped.

Joey whispered an apology to her and passed out, falling onto the grass at her feet with the rest of the dead.

Chapter 20

Alys

Harder. Push harder. Again, again. Move faster, be better, be stronger. Alys' mind mocked and encouraged her in equal measure, and in Jennifer's voice. Always the voice of her mother. It had become second nature, that voice driving her, empowering her. This is what she'd spent thousands of hours training for. This.

The years of torturing her muscles, taking the hits, falling, rising, again, again, again. *This was so worth it.*

She'd never felt so free, so alive. She'd never felt such purpose.

This. This is what she was made for.

With a scream of rage and joy she leapt at the next one, taking its head clean off with a single slash. Volleying the dried head, she marvelled at how light it felt as it struck her foot and bulleted off, straight into the face of an oncoming fresh Zom who staggered back. She felt like laughing. Instead she shoved her Sai through the temple of the next one, and the next, and began to clear herself some room to move. A few more inches, maybe a foot around her. Just a little bit more space free, unoccupied by the next Zom. Then she could really get going.

Chapter 21

Joey

Joey regained consciousness, becoming slowly aware that he still lay on the grass beneath her. *She hadn't left him.*

Whirling, jabbing her Sai, leaping and kicking, she was a lethal whirlwind of blows and strikes and death. Inches from his prone body she did what had to be done. That's what she always did. He rolled over from his back onto his side, curled his body inward and ripped off his right boot. One glance at the red stain blossoming out across the fabric of his sock from the big toe of his foot told him that it was all over. The nail had been bitten through. He watched the blood spread, detachedly noting to himself how like a poppy it looked with his toe at the centre of the blood flower.

Why is she still here?

Glancing across at his left hand, he noticed that an injury he'd taken there was bleeding freely also.

Trying to stand, he braced himself with the palm of his right hand pressed into the mud and blood, but found that his legs weren't listening and crumpled back to the ground. He tried twice more to stand before she kneed him in the shoulder, knocking him back to a curled position. She'd fought harder still and made a three-second gap in the fight to turn her attention to him. Three seconds was three times as many as she'd need, but that's how she was. Well prepared. He'd taught her that. They'd taught each other so much in the too-little time they'd spent together.

Instead of the terror he'd expected, a peaceful acceptance slid over him. He didn't raise his hands to protect himself and he didn't close his eyes. Placing one foot either side of him in a strike position, she raised her third Sai, the deadliest, swirled it around in her palm to a stabbing position and threw herself at him. As she struck he did close his eyes. Not for himself, not to welcome the black darkness he still missed from Mary King's Close, but for *her*. She shouldn't have to look in his eyes as she killed him. Silenced him.

Thank you, Alys, Joey's voice whispered inside his head. Outside, Joseph MacLeod was still.

"Aaaaaaargh."

Joey's upper body curled up, launching him onto his feet in response to the pain in his right foot. Alys was already back into her stride, whirling, showering her personal space with a hundred different killing blows, defending him as well as herself. Joey shook his confusion off and returned to the fight, ignoring the pain in his foot and his former toe, which Alys had severed and a Zom dressed as a fire-fighter had just made a quick meal of.

Reinvigorated, inspired by her bravery, by the risk she'd taken to try to save him from the infection spreading, and riding a wave of adrenaline, he steeled himself and fought harder than he'd ever done before. Together they pushed back the dead, stabbing and thrusting and bleeding from a million scratches, cuts and tears from rancid fingernails and calloused hands. They cleared a space and the dead began to thin out.

"Up there, Joey."

He turned, following Alys' Sai tip to a broad oak tree twenty feet to Alys' left.

"Think you can get up there?" She elbowed one of The Ringed in the forehead with the blade of her Sai along her forearm as she spoke.

A huge grin broke out on Joey's face as Alys began to count down.

"Three, two, one."

On one, Joey spun around in front of Alys and began sprinting at the tree, a painful limp blunting his usual speed. Using the fiery pain in his foot to fuel him, Joey shouldered six Zoms aside, one at a time. Reaching the trunk at almost full speed, he ran several steps vertically up the trunk and grabbed out for the lowest hanging branch that would hold him, crying out at the further damage done to his toe with the effort. Scooping his legs up after his hands, he landed smoothly astride the branch. Joey rose to his feet instantly and began scrambling further up the tree, coming to his knees in a ready position at a wide meeting place of two large branches.

He had fifty arrows at hand and didn't waste a single shot as he cleared a path for Alys out from the epicentre of the herd she still fought.

As Alys took her cue and took off at a sprint towards the Royal Infirmary, dispatching a few more Ringed as she ran, Joey fired his remaining arrows into some Zoms that shambled after her. He had no idea where he might find replacements for the arrows he'd spent, or if he might have the opportunity to recover the fifty that protruded from so many Zom heads in these woods, but they'd survive. That was all that mattered. Descending the tree, he ran after Alys, a little clumsily, due to the lack of a big toe on his right foot.

He caught up to Alys as they broke through some tangled greenery at the end of the cycle path and out onto the grounds to the infirmary. Joey flashed her a smile.

"That's a finger *and* a toe you owe me," he said, jabbing the stump of his middle finger at her in a rude gesture that had become their own private joke.

"Stop feeding them to Zoms, then," she replied, face breaking into a smile of her own.

She punched him in the usual spot and then shocked him for the second time that day by wrapping her arms around him. She pulled him close in an embrace he hadn't a hope of escaping, if he'd even wanted to. They held each other for a few long moments, each just happy to still have the other. Joey could have stayed there forever.

"What's that?" Alys suddenly broke off and moved nearer to the hospital grounds.

Having had his back to the hospital, Joey followed after her, noticing something shining in the distance.

"Is that.... a light?" Alys stammered.

"An electric light?"

Joey shrugged. He'd never seen one before. Neither had she, so how could they be sure?

Peering deeper into the darkness, he spotted something and took Alys by the hand, guiding her a few feet on towards the building shapes in the distance. Reaching out with his hand, the one that held hers, they made contact together with a very large, very tall, and very strong steel fence which sealed the hospital grounds.

After their encounter with the massive herd of The Ringed, which had so clearly originated from the hospital, they'd expected the grounds around it to be overrun also. It seemed that someone had cleared the hospital compound and secured it with a very impressive perimeter fence. It was far taller and stronger than any that surrounded their own communities and more closely resembled the outer fence-line around the city. The one that prevented the survivors from leaving. That meant safety from the pursuing herd.

"We need to get in here," Joey said.

After searching around for less than ten minutes, they found a hole, dug under the fence from their side, leading into the compound.

A darkness spread over Joey's face.

"He's already here," he said softly.

"It might be someone else?" Alys offered.

Joey bent down and ran his hands along the trench and under the fence-line. Pulling at something, he lifted a scrap of chequered material from golfer's trousers for Alys to see.

"It's him. Let's go."

Being smaller than Bracha, neither had any difficulty slipping under the fence-line.

"What's the plan?" Alys asked.

Joey shrugged.

"Hole-up 'til morning?"

"You give us the advantage at night." Alys gestured towards his eyes and then flicked his right ear. "Bat-boy."

Despite the tension, they both laughed.

"Okay. But something's not right. There's a weird sound here I haven't heard before. You hear it?"

Alys cocked her head.

"A kind of humming?"

"Yeah, but it's not an animal. I don't know what it is. Let's find that, and then see about our favourite golfer. That okay?"

Alys agreed and fell in behind him, signalling that he should lead the way. Pressing against buildings and using greenery as cover, they slowly followed the sound from one end of the compound to the other. As they moved, Joey scanned around constantly. Their path was taking them closer to the light they'd seen earlier.

"Weird," Alys whispered.

Joey jerked his chin upwards in a questioning gesture.

"There are no Zoms at all inside their fences."

Joey realised that she was right. He was so accustomed to the presence of The Ringed that once he registered that he couldn't see or hear one anywhere around, he felt instantly uncomfortable. It didn't feel right, this silence outside.

Silence in Mary King's Close he was familiar with, but outside? The soundtrack was all wrong without the shuffle-groan of the dead.

Alys reached out, taking his hand and squeezing it to reassure him that it felt odd to her also.

"Let's go." He moved off, a little more alert than before. "We're close," he whispered to her. "I can feel the vibrations from it."

"Me too."

Joey and Alys slipped around the edge of the Chancellor's Building and stopped dead as they spotted the source of the strange sound they'd followed.

Both recognised it instantly from pictures they'd seen as kids. It was a relic from the past. It should be silent and rusted and still. But there it was; a huge, fully-functional generator, chugging away, pouring out electricity, sending the energy along so many cables leading to the main hospital wing in which a row of six electric lights shone bright as suns through fully intact glass windows.

Interlude

Fraser Donnelly

Pressing his thumb to the keypad on the door to his apartment, Fraser held his anger in check as the scanner slid over his fingerprint and chirped cheerfully for him to enter. He threw his coat onto the floor as he stepped inside, slamming the door loudly behind him. Leaning his back against the inside of his apartment door, he let loose a stream of very colourful expletives and some very impractical suggestions for what his superiors could do to themselves.

He felt better for getting it out of his system, here in the privacy of his apartment. In the boardroom, of course, he'd been supremely calm and confident. *Yes, sir... Have you considered that, sir... Here's my plan, sir.* He silently thanked… whoever that they'd eventually sanctioned his idea.

Ignoring the growl from his stomach, he strode towards the drinks dispenser by the refrigerator.

"Glenmorangie. No ice," he barked at the automation.

Seconds later he'd downed the golden liquid and ordered another, whilst enjoying the pleasant burn from the last. By the time he'd had his third, a double this time, Fraser already felt mellower and much more confident that events would play out the way he wished them to.

Laughing as loudly as he'd sworn minutes before, he clicked the fingers of his right hand, mentally snapping his attention back. Taking a seat at his computer array, he pressed his back deep into the luxurious leather, appreciating the quality.

The Brits knew how to do a big comfortable, leather chair. Bull's leather, that's the key. Bull's, not cow's. The Brits, they knew that cow's leather was covered in bloody stretch marks.

Fraser made a gesture and a holo-screen popped up in front of him. He hadn't spoken to that moron Paterson for a few hours. He couldn't stand the man, but he was surprisingly discreet and kept Fraser appraised of events in the quarantined city when he couldn't reach a holo-screen of his own. The last word he'd had on the pair of teens was that they were camped on a cycle path en route to the Royal Infirmary. It was a problem and one that he'd had to move swiftly to deal with.

Issuing orders for the teams at the Infirmary to clear out and that all duties be suspended, Fraser was currently juggling one too many balls for his liking. The official reason he'd given his superiors and the team on-site was that fences had been damaged by the infected and several of the creatures were roaming the hospital grounds. Several of the senior employees had complained that they'd be leaving assignments, important projects behind, some of which couldn't be recovered. Some worried about equipment.

All of the cameras placed by The Corporation throughout the plague-ridden city to monitor the survivors fed into the Royal Infirmary and were then bounced out via satellite to the outside world; to Corporation Headquarters. The outpost had been run on a skeleton crew for years. Discretion was the key. For that discretion and for the risk they took in entering the quarantine zone, the men and women who manned the Infirmary station were paid handsomely. Fraser Donnelly reminded them who they worked for and how fortunate they were to be paid such a lucrative salary. He also enquired as to whether they'd be happy to be devoured by the infected. They left without further complaint.

It was another necessary lie with Joseph MacLeod and his friend making their way towards the hospital, and one that had been difficult to sell to his superiors. Difficult, but not impossible. The Corporation had a blanket policy: no resident of Edinburgh could be permitted to discover the outpost on the hospital grounds or its purpose. Anyone who had stumbled into the grounds in the past had been permanently taken care of. When his superiors had discovered that the teens were headed towards the outpost, the order to eliminate was given immediately. Thanks to Paterson's vigil, Donnelly had gotten word of their path slightly ahead of them and had had time to prepare.

Donnelly had asked that the teens be allowed to enter the grounds, but only after the staff had been evacuated, suggesting that they'd find an empty compound with no trace of the cure they sought. After that, they'd simply go home. It was the humane way to deal with the situation and an opportunity to have the kids spread word that the area was dead. The compound would have to be closed temporarily and the infected cleared out anyway. They might as well allow the teens the time to explore, conclude that there was no cure and that the compound was as abandoned as the rest of their city.

It had been a close vote, but the board trusted his judgement. Fraser had worked for thirty years to become CEO and had proven his worth and commitment many times over. Now all he had to do was ensure that those kids didn't discover anything they shouldn't and cleared the hell out by morning.

Swiping again at the air, the holo-screen changed at his command to an image from earlier in the day. Fraser watched Joseph and the girl fight their way through an impossible number of infected. He was mesmerised by them both. Neither would leave the other, neither would fall. It was an incredible sight to behold. Eventually, they made their way under the fence to the hospital and had stumbled across an office block, fully-lit, and the generator chugging away.

"Goddammit!" Fraser threw his empty tumbler across the room.

He glanced at his wristwatch, formerly his father's. Coverage was normally twenty-four hours, but with the evacuation of the outpost and the loss of power to the site, the feed had been terminated for a twelve-hour period. Only the private feed to the individual board members' computers remained active. Generally he was likely to be the only one watching at this late hour. He said a silent prayer that this would hold true, but there was nothing he could do. Either someone else on the board was watching or they weren't, it was out of his control.

What bloody fool left that one, single generator whirring away, and all those bloody lights on?

It didn't matter. The teens had seen the generator and the lights. His only option was to get them out of the compound somehow, destroy any footage and hope that no one else was watching a private feed before the main generators kicked back into life in the morning.

Returning his eyes to the holo-screen, he made a very slow clockwise motion with his index finger and watched in fast-forward as the pair walked around the generator for some moments and then locked themselves into a supply shed for the night.

Fraser pulled the finger sharply back, pausing the image on the screen. He examined the boy's face. He was a handsome kid, determined beyond reason and so very... so very... Fraser reclined back into his chair, pushed the thought from his mind and drank a large mouthful from his new glass as he took in the familiar face which was now filling his holo-screen.

Noticing something, a shadow perhaps at the bottom of the paused screen, he rotated his finger clockwise again, slowly moving frame by frame until a man came into focus. Sitting with his back pressed up against the shed door, smiling, listening to every word from inside, Bracha sat, stroking his golf club.

Fraser left his bull's leather chair whirling and tore out of his apartment, headed for the corporation's headquarters at 30 St Mary Axe, The Gherkin, London.

Chapter 22

Alys

"I think we should search the building in the morning, especially those lighted areas." Alys felt her heart race a little when she mentioned the lights they'd seen. It was like a miracle. Electricity. But one that dripped with threat and confusion rather than wonder.

Joey didn't answer right away. He was clearly not keen at all on going anywhere near the lit building, having insisted on them holing up for the night to plan their next move and tend to his wounded foot. He was also clearly choosing his words very carefully.

"I have a bad feeling about this place, Alys." He subconsciously cracked each of his knuckles in sequence as he spoke. "How can they be running a generator? There hasn't been any usable fuel for years. Why is the place empty of humans and of Ringed? Obviously most of the herd we fought through in Hawkshill Wood came from here. It's so well-fenced, it's obviously been set up to keep a large group of people in and any number of Zoms out. So where the hell is everyone?"

Alys shrugged.

"The only way to answer any of those questions is to search the place, Joey."

He harrumphed to himself and sat in the corner of the tool shed, arms wrapped around bent knees.

Alys mirrored his pose against the opposite wall.

"Look, we came all this way, it'd be insane to leave without seeing what's here." Joey rested his head on his lap, avoiding eye contact. She picked up a little stone from the ground at threw it at the top of his head.

"Ow," he complained, rubbing the spot she'd hit.

Alys ignored his protest and continued.

"Whether Bracha is really here or not, whether there's really a cure in that building or just dusty old desks, beds and chairs, we'll only find out by going in there first thing in the morning. Four hours or so, we'll go slowly, carefully. There's nothing we can't handle in that hospital. Look at what we overcame on the way here."

"Bracha's more dangerous than any group of Zoms, Alys. You know that."

"I agree," she said. "Which is why we'll take him on together. As a unit. He can't handle both of us at once, no matter how skilled he is. If we come across him…"

Joey's eyes went hard suddenly and bored into her. "We'll find him. There's no way I'm leaving here now without finishing it with him."

Alys swallowed.

"*When* we come across him, you have to trust me to go in and engage him at close-quarters." She expected an argument but received a curt nod in agreement instead. Alys suppressed a smile and continued. "You hang back and take a position where you can pepper him with arrows every time a clean shot appears. That's how we play this."

"Only one problem, Alys." Joey tipped his empty quiver upside-down, bringing a colourful remark from Alys.

"We either have to go back and retrieve some arrows or risk getting in each other's way by both engaging him at close quarters," Alys said. She didn't look pleased with either option.

"I say we both go in for him. We're a good enough team," Joey replied.

"No. We're not," Alys said bluntly. "When we play to our strengths and work together, we're good enough. Your bow and my hand to hand skills are how we work effectively... I'm sorry Joey, but as good as you've gotten, you just aren't good enough to go up against a guy like Bracha. Especially with that foot injury. I've trained my whole life and even I'm not one hundred percent certain that I can take this guy alone."

Joey accepted her assessment despite looking a little miffed. Alys rose to her feet and walked over to where Joey still crouched. Coming down to his eye level, she told him, "Joey, I'm scared of Bracha. I reckon he'd give my mum a run for her money."

Joey's eyebrows rose in response. He clearly didn't think anyone was capable of giving Jennifer much trouble. He was wrong in this instance.

Bracha knew what he was doing; he was lethally clever, infinitely patient and supremely confident in his own skills. With his blades, Bracha used the simplest of weapons. Weapons that meant close-up action, and that he used with finesse. The golfer's outfit and the silly club-twirling were all just a ridiculous act, contrived to make people underestimate him.

Even his accent was faked, designed to elicit trust in or disdain for him. Anything that would make his target drop their guard. He didn't fight or kill to survive; he didn't act to assert supremacy or dominance over individuals. He did it for the sport, to test himself.

Bracha lived for the kill. That he'd killed Jock whilst Joey slept beside him, doing so silently, skilfully enough that he hadn't woken someone with Joey's senses, told Alys everything about the man's motives and his skillset. The act of keeping Joey alive so that he might pursue him to avenge his mentor told Alys that Bracha was an arrogant bastard who treated death like a game. That was his weakness.

Alys stood once more offering Joey her hand. Joey rose, bringing his face closer to hers than he intended. She was still marginally taller than him and looked down at his eyes as he stood less than an inch from her. He looked concerned, but resolved.

"Let's get some sleep and make our way over to the edge of Hawkshill Wood in the morning. See if we can get you a dozen or so arrows back from where we fought today. With any luck The Ringed will have wandered off, or followed something else away from the ones we silenced."

A resigned look fell over Joey's face.

"All right, Alys. Let's do it your way."

Ten minutes later they were spooned against the bitter cold.

"Alys? You awake?"

"Yeah."

"You've never told me what happened to your dad. Why did he leave The Gardens with all the other men?"

Alys stayed silent for a few minutes, trying to form an explanation. Finally she told him the truth.

"I've no idea. One day he was there, the next he was gone. And he never came back."

"I'm sorry."

"Not your fault, s'just the way it is. Go to sleep, Joey."

"If we do find a cure, what can we do with it?" he asked.

Having spent her time focused on getting to the hospital, finding the cure, if it existed, and dealing with Bracha, she hadn't really considered that outcome.

"I don't have a bloody clue." She laughed. "But, it would be a good problem to have, eh?"

Joey pulled himself closer into her back, arm over her side, hand resting on her abdomen. She could feel him smelling her hair.

"Aye, a good problem. G'night, Alys."

Ten minutes after he'd replied, despite the discomfort of the stone floor and the cold, despite what lay ahead of them, they were both fast asleep.

Curled together in a warm unit they were unaware of the movement of shadows passing across the light breaking through the gap at the bottom of the locked shed door. The round handle turned clockwise then anti-clockwise, without a sound, and then stayed still until morning light sneaked under the door.

Chapter 23

James Kelly

Sitting on the trunk of a fallen tree, James swore for perhaps the fifteenth time as he checked his watch once again. *Four a.m.* Despite the thermals he wore and two layers on top, the cold was creeping into his bones, sending nerve pain through the joints of his knees and stiffening his vertebrae. Bracha was two hours later than his message had stated. The sun would rise soon. James would give him another half an hour, then he was leaving.

James stood and began marching to and fro along the trail that had led him to the secluded clearing at the edge of Drum Wood in an effort to get his blood flowing. He'd slipped out from his little bungalow in the cul-de-sac that formed The Exalted's camp after

Somna had retired for the night, deciding that he'd rather not explain his trip unless he had to. Somna wasn't exactly Bracha's biggest fan. The meeting place Bracha had selected was far too close to The Exalted's base for James' liking, but Bracha's message had insisted that it was urgent.

When he'd first arrived in the clearing he'd had to deal with a pair of Zoms. One male and one female. He'd crashed the end of his Bo-staff through each of their skulls, not bothering to perform the ritual expected of him by The Exalted's dogma. The thought of Bracha catching him in the process of performing the ritual was unbearable.

He hadn't seen Bracha for almost two years and would have preferred to keep it that way, considering the circumstances in which the bushy-haired madman had departed their community. They had been friends at one time, best friends actually, despite Bracha being perhaps the most dangerous killer (after Somna) amongst a community of killers, rapists and lunatics. James owed him his life and as such couldn't ignore Bracha when he sent word that help was required, no matter the danger to him. If he didn't appear soon, though, James would have to get back into Drum Woods before there were any questions, or worse, waiting for him.

Suddenly aware that he wasn't alone, James reached for the Bo-staff he'd left by the fallen tree and spun around to face a grinning Bracha who'd slipped into the clearing.

"Never could sneak up on you, old boy," Bracha grinned at him.

"Where the hell have you been?"

Bracha cocked an eyebrow.

"I do apologise for my tardiness, James. I've had a spot of trouble."

James looked his former friend over. Taking in the relative stiffness of the movement of his right arm and the missing eye, he smiled and asked, "Finally met someone better with a blade than yourself?"

Bracha raised his nose into the air, giving a derisory snort.

"I hardly think so, James."

He pointed at his lower and then upper arm.

"This was the result of a teenager from The Gardens' skilled use of Sai."

Bracha scanned his face for a reaction before poking a finger at his missing eye, the socket now filled with a brightly-coloured marble painted with a yellow smiling face.

"This, by a teenaged boy from The Brotherhood with a bow."

This time James did allow his reaction to show.

"One of The Brotherhood? He left The Close and lives on the surface?" His surprise was genuine.

"Oh yes. And he's quite skilled." Bracha squeaked a finger across surface of his right-eye-cum-smiley-faced-marble.

Have you visited the city-centre?" James asked.

Bracha gave a non-committal shrug.

"Not really... but I plan to get acquainted with the lovely ladies of The Gardens in the near future." Bracha pulled his stiletto blade and began picking at his nails with the tip. "You've been there, haven't you?" Bracha said.

James shrugged. "Not really." He was trying to antagonise Bracha, but didn't really expect his ex-friend to rise to his attempt.

"And your master, Somna? So convinced that the city-centre communities were no longer there. Wasn't it you who gave him that intelligence?"

James didn't bother shrugging this time, rather he spent his concentration on keeping his facial expression indifferent.

Bracha picked away at the nails of his right hand, giving James a clear view of an arrow-tip-shaped scar through his palm.

Bracha caught him glancing at it.

"Oh yes, our archer. Quite skilled, as I said."

He must be, to have injured you twice, James thought. *But not as skilled as the girl, she had to have gotten in close to break those bones.*

Relaxing his posture, James resumed his seated position once more on the fallen tree.

Bracha strolled over to where the pair of Zoms lay, one toppled on top of the other.

"These are very fresh-looking, James. Recent additions to the Tribe, perhaps?"

James ignored his questions.

"What do you want, Bracha?"

"As blunt as ever, I see. I suppose that's why you succeeded me as *his* number two. Not much cunning about you, is there, James?" Bracha placed his stiletto back into whatever concealed place it had been drawn from. His injuries hadn't dampened his speed… much.

"The archer and his little girlfriend…" Bracha flexed his stiff right arm subconsciously at mentioning her. "They're in my way."

"So what? Kill them then," James said without disturbing the passiveness of his expression.

Bracha smiled that cold smile of his. The one that showed off his perfectly straight, very white teeth, one of the few signs of the wealth and privilege he'd been raised in that he still wore.

"I'm not really up for that right now. Some help would be appreciated." He indicated his injured arm.

James shook his head. "No. If you have a problem with those kids, fix it for yourself or just leave them alone."

Bracha sighed. "They're at the hospital."

James' heart sank. "Then they'll be dead soon enough."

"Actually, the entire compound has been shut down, at least at the moment. Has that ever happened before?"

James thought for a moment.

"Maybe, around six years ago. It went dark for twelve hours, nightfall to sunrise, and then back to business as usual. Somna got word of it beforehand and was instructed to discourage anyone who might see the closure as an opportunity to scale the fences."

"Instructed by whom?" Bracha asked.

James shrugged. "You know who. The Corporation."

"Somna still receives supplies, medicines and intel from them in return for keeping the hospital's outer perimeter clean of intruders?"

Another non-committal shrug from James.

"I didn't see any of your people anywhere in or around the compound. Obviously this close-down wasn't planned." Bracha smiled.

He pulled his coat tightly and drew his golf club, twirling it playfully around with his left hand. It was a sign that the conversation was over and he was leaving.

"I'd best get back before my little love-birds wake up. Do I have your word that you won't inform Somna of my presence? I promise that I'll be long gone by midday. After I've seen to my young city-centre friends."

"Why don't you just leave them to it? Wait until you're healed before you engage them?" James asked.

Bracha's face darkened. "You know what's in there, James. I can't let them find it."

"The cure?" James asked. "That's a bloody myth, Bracha. You can't honestly believe in it."

Bracha gave no answer. Instead he turned and melted into the dark foliage.

James sat, staring into the dark woods for a few moments. *A girl from The Gardens, a boy from The Brotherhood.* The words replayed through his head. *A fighter. Expert with Sai, an archer.*

James was on his feet one minute after Bracha departed, sprinting for Drum Woods and Somna's bungalow.

Chapter 24

Joey

Eyes glued shut from sleep-snot, Joey reached up with his left hand and rubbed some of the graininess away. The right arm he didn't budge. Now able to open his eyes, he peeked through the murk looking at Alys sleeping peacefully, her back to him, head resting on his right arm. Despite his arm having gone numb hours before and a warm ain emanating from his foot wound, Joey couldn't recall ever feeling so comfortable.

Lifting his head a little he noticed that a thin frosted dew covered their clothes, boots and hair. They'd best get on the move… in a moment. As he grinned to himself and settled his head back down, a thunderous rattle echoed through the shed from the locked door.

"Little Pigs, Little Pigs... Let me in." Bracha's mocking voice was full of amusement.

Instantly on their feet, they drew their weapons, Alys choosing her two blunt Sai and blinking the blurriness from her eyes. Joey drew his blades too, not that he had any choice. A quiver-full of arrows lay two hundred yards into the woods. They may as well have been on Jupiter.

"You go first, crash the door and step aside. I'll see if it's clear to move out," Joey whispered.

It was a horrible position to be in. If he'd had his bow, getting both of them through the door safely would be a whole lot simpler, but that wasn't an option.

Alys quietly unlocked the door and shoved it out, rolling her right shoulder along the wall to leave the open doorway clear. Nothing came through so Joey dived outside. Tucking into a roll that brought him up onto his feet in a ready stance a metre away from the shed, he called to Alys.

"Clear."

Alys shot through the door taking position so that they stood back to back. All of Joey's senses were on maximum, but it was a shrill state of alertness. He wasn't at his best in full daylight and found it difficult to blink his eyes into full focus.

"You see him anywhere?" Alys asked.

Before Joey could answer, a fire exit door swung open from a building further down the street on which they stood. Bracha's red hair came through, followed by the rest of him. He'd clearly expected Joey to be armed with his bow and hadn't hung around outside the tool shed. They'd caught a lucky break.

Bracha greeted them like old friends.

"Kids! How delightful to see you both."

He stood grinning manically at them for several long moments, waiting for a reply he wouldn't get.

Standing in the middle of the road, arms and hands spread to his sides, he began to take a few slow steps towards them.

"Of course, you really shouldn't be here." He indicated the hospital compound as he took several more steps. He was assessing them, deciding if he could engage both of them. He thought that he was in control.

"How's the eye?" Joey called, straining to make out what Bracha currently had sitting in his right eye socket.

A flicker of something dark passed over Bracha's face for a moment but was quickly replaced by his jovial, kindly uncle expression.

"Oh, I got a nicer one. So kind of you to be concerned for me though, Joseph."

His smile broadened.

"Did you give the padre a nice sending-off? Some nice words spoken over his grave, maybe a few close friends sharing a pleasant meal and exchanging anecdotes about the old boy?"

"Ignore him," Alys whispered out the corner of her mouth.

"What's that, my dear? Oh, how rude of me. I forgot to ask about your dear cousin. Stephanie, wasn't it? Lovely girl, she's keeping well, I hope?" Bracha winked at her with his marble-eye. "Perhaps I'll visit with her? Once we conclude our… meeting. Oh, and once the cure has been disposed of. It's through here, y'know." He nodded into the doorway he'd come through. "Found it earlier, but I had a little trouble opening the container." He smiled his reptilian smile, raising his right arm.

Alys grinned humourlessly, noting the lack of mobility in the limb.

Joey had had enough of his words, and threw him a line Jock had used to antagonise opponents.

"Are you gonna bark all day, or are you gonna bite?"

Bracha gave him a pitying look.

"As you wish, young archer."

In a flash he disappeared through the open door.

Both Alys and Joey shot after him. Sprinting through the doorway they heard his footsteps echo along the corridor. They skidded to a full halt before entering, but not out of fear or caution since Bracha was well into the building from the sound of things. What alarmed them was how clean the corridor was. How… white.

They'd never been inside a building with artificial light, or one that didn't have plants or moss creeping along the walls and floors. Their footsteps felt different on the hardness of the tiles. Their voices sounded all wrong, bouncing off the bare walls. It was an alien world to them, this one simple corridor.

Alys turned to him. "It's so unnatural-looking."

Joey didn't know what to say, so gave her hand a squeeze, offering reassurance and gaining the same from touching her.

They stepped further along the corridor, instinctively lightening their footsteps to counteract the noise of their boots on the pristine floor. A few metres along the corridor, they noticed a map of the building.

Instead of wards, it was filled with offices, labs and tech rooms, all labelled neatly on a graphic painted onto the wall. Both of them were unnerved by how impossibly new everything was.

"Do you think this place has been sealed shut since the plague broke?" Joey asked.

Alys shook her head. "Can't have been, or it'd be full of dampness, bugs, moss and God knows what by now."

Her eyes widened as the realisation hit.

"People have been here, recently. This place is being used for something by people. People from out there." She jabbed a thumb over her shoulder at the general direction of the fence-line.

"That can't be true, Alys. Nobody would come through the outer fences. They don't want to be infected. Something else must be happening. Maybe it's something to do with The Exalted? They're in the area."

"I don't know, Joey. Have you ever seen any community live like this, with access to electricity?"

Bracha stepped around a turn at the far end of the corridor. The fake, cheery demeanour was gone. He had a blade in each hand, one of them the stiletto he'd killed Jock and maimed Steph with. The sight of him, and *it*, made Joey have to work very hard to stay calm.

"I assume that the padre told you about The Exalted, Joseph?"

Joey didn't reply. He didn't have to. Bracha had already read something in his body language or facial expression that confirmed for him that this was the case.

Bracha twirled the stiletto blade around in his fingers in the same manner he did with his golf club. He was clearly deciding what to say.

"This place isn't theirs." He jerked his head to the right, indicating the building.

Joey and Alys remained still, but ready. *Let him talk,* they were both thinking.

"She's right." He pointed the tip of his stiletto at Alys. "This place is normally shut down, inaccessible. On a normal day, merely approaching the fences will get you executed." A toothy grin spread across his face. "It is a complete disgrace that I couldn't access this building before. My grandmother opened it, you know?"

Bracha noticed the puzzled look on both of their faces, quickly replaced by indifference. He waved his hand as though dismissing his own words as unimportant.

"Ancient history."

Suddenly his face morphed into a perfect mask of hatred.

"I picked a good day to attempt stealthy entry. It seems the place is in close-down, maybe only for a few more hours, maybe minutes."

Bracha threw a square, white padded pack with a large red cross emblazoned on it towards them.

Joey watched it skitter along the smooth tiles and put a boot on top of it when it came to him.

"I found that at the location I'd been told I'd find the cure. Open it." Bracha spat the words.

Stealing a quick glance at Alys, he noticed the eagerness in her eyes. *Do it*, they said. Joey unzipped the bag around its lid.

Empty.

"So there it is: your cure."

Bracha almost disappeared in a blur of speed as he ran towards them. With the corridor so narrow, they weren't able to fight as a unit. Rather Alys would engage, perform a few sequences, then allow Joey to move in. They fought like this, alternating attacks, delivering kicks, elbows and punches. Weapon slashes and strikes all thrown at a variety of angles and in a myriad of styles. After two exchanges lasting five seconds, Alys knew that they could beat him, but only because his arm didn't have a full range of motion and only together.

She stepped up her attack, spreading more blows to his right where he couldn't defend effectively. He wasn't tiring but he was getting frustrated at his own ineffectiveness. She didn't improve his mood when she delivered a vicious backhand strike to his face, breaking his nose with a sickening crunch.

Following the momentum of her swing she spun around, allowing Joey to step through and launch a front kick into his gonads. Bracha went down instantly, projecting a plume of bright green vomit onto the white tiles as he collapsed. *Vagus nerve*, Joey thought, stepping back whilst Alys hammered her knee into the back of his neck, smashing his face into the tiles and breaking his mandible. She systematically used the heavy-butted handles of her Sai in overhand blows to break one hand, then the other, followed by a series of blows to the back of his ribcage. Joey watched her strikes flash along, breaking five of his ribs.

"Try talking now, you bastard," she spat at him, rising to her feet.

Joey fished out a handful of plastic cable ties from his pockets and handed a few to Alys.

She looked puzzled. "We should just kill him."

"I don't disagree, but I want a look around this place first. See if there's anything useful, or something that can tell us more about whoever runs this place. According to him." Joey kicked at the unconscious Bracha.

"We don't have much time. I want to know more about this compound before we leave and, like it or not, this piece of trash knows more than we do."

Alys didn't look happy. Pulling the USB drive Jock had given him from his pocket, he held it in an open palm for her to see.

She nodded her agreement and helped him restrain Bracha's limp body by wrists and feet and attach him to a large, immovable iron radiator.

"Let's make it quick," she said

A door immediately to Bracha's right had a sign labelling it as *Main Feed Router.* That sounded like something technical they wouldn't understand and so they headed the other direction, along the corridor.

They made their way through a series of offices, trying not to waste time staring at the electrical equipment they saw in each space. Neither had any idea what most of it was, but Alys had seen a photo of a laptop in a magazine she'd read as a kid and picked one up for Joey in the third room they visited. It'd been plugged into an electrical socket and had a little green light buzzing on its front face before she'd unplugged it. They hoped that it meant a full charge in its battery, but it was inconsequential until they found someone who could use it. *Maybe Bracha.*

Almost every room, and corridor, had the same stylised logo on its walls.

UKBC

Neither of them recognised it. The logo was also on mugs of unfinished coffee, stationery and some lab coats. It seemed people had left in a hurry, and recently.

Having searched all of the offices and taken everything they recognised as useful, which was very little, the pair made their way back to the corridor they started from.

Alys handed him the laptop. "Time to get some use out of that monster."

Joey took the device and made his way along to where Bracha still lay, strapped to the radiator.

Chapter 25

James Kelly

James looked along the group of Exalted, lined along the fence that looped around the Royal Infirmary compound on Little France Crescent. Each of them looked relaxed, but determined. Almost none of the fifty who had assembled here today on Somna's command had been at the hospital the last time Somna was called upon to defend its fences.

Most had never been near the compound, despite its close proximity to The Exalted's base at Drum Woods. Somna's deal with The Corporation didn't allow for their presence beyond the Dalkeith Road fences, unless ordered so by The Corporation. James had no idea how The Corporation communicated with Somna – he'd never seen any contact take place

– but he was fairly certain that none had in the hours since he'd told Somna of Bracha's presence and the absence of personnel at the hospital. Somna was acting on his own initiative, James was sure of that.

James had torn into Somna's bungalow within minutes of leaving his meeting with Bracha. Finding his leader praying at the feet of their King, he'd waited patiently for the ritual to end before seeking Somna's attention. As Somna knelt at the base of his King's altar, James moved his eyes over the scene in front of him as he decided exactly what he should tell him.

As always, the King was bound to bamboo poles. Snarling at his follower, the King was held in the pose he'd used as his logo when he'd been a footballer: one arm out in front, the other behind for balance, one leg planted and the other in mid swing. The posture of this footballer taking his famous free kicks, forever preserved in the form of the undead remains of the once famous man. It was a sick parody of the image the footballer had presented before The Fall. Power, money, fame, skill, determination; all represented by the sick pose he was held unnaturally in by the infection in his cells and the ropes on his limbs.

The presence of the King never failed to sicken James. Unlike the rest of The Exalted, James Kelly was not now and had never been a true believer. His loyalty to the tribe was one of necessity rather than devotion.

He didn't subscribe to the tribe's beliefs that cleansing the city of all life, as communicated to Somna by this King, was their holy mission. He did know a winning side when he saw one, though, and the pragmatist he'd been since leaving the city-centre so many years before whispered to him that Somna and his followers couldn't be stopped.

Somna, of course, knew that he didn't buy into The Exalted's religion and tolerated James' lack of belief because of his combat skills and farming knowledge. When Bracha's unsuccessful coup had been ended and Bracha had escaped punishment by fleeing the tribe, James had taken his best friend's position as Somna's right hand. He'd served ten years as Somna's lieutenant. Ten years.

Shifting his eyes once more, to Somna this time, he reflected on what a truly hideous sight Somna was. Dressed in black, worn biker-leathers he stood at almost six-seven in height. His skin was covered in a network of tattoos, all of which meant something to him or was a trophy, a reminder of each soul he'd *saved*. His trophies took the form of small ravens. He had hundreds of them etched permanently into his skin as a mark of his dedication to his King and of his success. All of The Exalted did this in celebration of the lives they'd sacrificed to their King.

James had only one raven, etched in flight under his right eye. A permanent tear.

Somna wore his black hair long, tightly wrapped in a sheik-like bun and fixed in place with wire at the crown of his head. Blackest of all his features were his eyes. So dark, like pools of black ink, no emotion. Nothing, not anger, fear, love or regret, ever showed in them. They belonged to a shark rather than a man. They also lacked the frame of upper or lower eyelids having been removed by his own hand "to better serve my King and watch my flock," *as he said.*

The very worst of Somna's appearance was also the one aspect that seemed most out of place. Around his waist hung a bum-bag, a fanny-pack, with the legend *I Love Edinburgh* in bright neon orange lettering. Inside were the other trophies he took from his victims, the ones he cut from them when only his trusted few lieutenants were present. A festering pack filled with the putrefied eyelids of hundreds.

Somna finished his prayers and fished a little bottle of self-made serum from his pocket. Holding the bottle above his permanently open eyes, he waited patiently as a few drops of the moisturising liquid fell. The muscles around his eyes contracted, still attempting to engage the blink reflex, unaware that they no longer held eyelids to flick over his exposed eyeballs. Somna rolled his eyes around in their sockets, face pointing to the ceiling, as he spoke.

"What can I do for you today, Jimmy?" His voice was entirely at odds with his appearance, being gentle, seductive even. Always calm.

James told him of his encounter with Bracha, explaining that he had been hunting in the woods when stumbling across the former lieutenant.

"What a coincidence," Somna said gently.

James held his poker face and continued. When Somna discovered that the hospital fences had been breached and the compound itself seemingly evacuated, he calmly rounded up fifty or so men within minutes and set off for Little France.

James had no idea whether the teens were still in the area, but whatever the case, it was out of his hands. Bracha had to be silenced. If Somna were to discover from him the extent to which James had lied to him about the status of the city-centre, he expected one more raven on Somna's skin would be his legacy. He followed his master out into the morning frost and aided a silent prayer for the children he may have just murdered to protect his own secrets.

Looking along at Somna standing on the perimeter of the hospital boundary on Little France Crescent, James watched the leader of The Exalted *converse* with their King, who had been carried to Little France on his platform, still in his perverted pose, half-deflated ball at his foot.

Somna threw his arms up suddenly. "We will have the traitor, Bracha, delivered unto us this very morning," he announced. "Our heavenly King assures me."

A ripple of excitement from the gathered men; James could almost taste the adrenaline surging through the gathered monsters.

Somna strolled calmly towards James and leaned in close, voice a whisper.

"If you feel any lingering loyalty to Bracha, best that you leave now, Jimmy."

A thousand memories rushed through James Kelly's mind in that moment. He had known the man who was now called Bracha for most of his life. They'd met in boarding school. They'd joined the army together. Two tours in Afghanistan. He'd become a member of the man's team of personal guards. He was there with his friend on the day the city fell. They could have left days before, a chopper had been sent, but *he* wanted to stay.

With his ruddy-red face and ginger hair, he'd told James, "This is the world now, and it's a damn sight more interesting than the one we've waded through all these years."

James and one other personal guard, Cammy, had stayed out of loyalty, out of duty. They'd followed their friend as he descended into madness. Cammy left soon after. James had stayed too long and finally abandoned him when he'd joined Somna's insanity and taken the name Bracha. James wept for his friend and grew to hate the monster who wore his appearance like a twisted suit.

He'd gone his own way. At one point he'd lived in the city-centre, joining Cammy there. They'd made a life there and had helped establish a little farming community. They'd found a sort of peace amongst the wandering grey people who roamed the city streets eternally. And then they found themselves banished from there also. Cammy had been bitten within weeks of leaving the centre. For all James knew, he wandered the streets of the city to this day. He hadn't had the heart to put him out of his misery.

Returning once more to Somna's compound to find his final friend, out of loyalty, out of need, only Bracha was there by then. Not a shred of the decent man his friend had been remained. But Bracha was all he had left so he'd had to make do until his grasp exceeded his reach and Bracha challenged Somna, making James choose between Somna and his friend.

James coughed. "I haven't felt anything for him since you gave him that name. Do what you have to do."

Somna smiled and returned to his King's altar to commune with his god.

Interlude

Fraser Donnelly

Three interns shot through into the control booth at Corporation House.

"Mr Donnelly's here. He's coming up, right now."

The shift manager, Stevie Trewartha, blinked. A long blink, the kind that came after four hours of sitting in a chair, no matter how luxurious, editing hours of footage through the night.

Stevie rubbed at his bloodshot eyes with the heel of his palms, took a long pull from the cold contents of his mug and painted on an expression of annoyance.

"Don't be ridiculous. Donnelly wouldn't come anywhere near this building. He can access everything he needs from home."

Intern number one – Stevie, hadn't bothered to learn their names – interrupted. "That's not strictly true, sir. There are several high-end and remote functions that not even..."

Stevie shot him a look, silencing him.

"Is he for real?" he asked intern number two.

The quieter of the interns, number two, merely nodded.

Intern one piped up again. "Sir, I assure you, he's right behind us."

Stevie stood. "It's McGinley, isn't it? He put you up to this."

Stevie left the main control room and scanned around the deserted main floor.

"Out you come, McGinley, I'm onto you."

The elevator beeped and Stevie launched himself over to the opening doors, stopping a foot short of a very irate-looking Fraser Donnelly.

"Out. And take those two clowns with you."

Stevie didn't want to argue, he really didn't, but in his time at The Corporation, fifteen years this July, he'd had it drummed into him: *never leave unauthorised personnel alone in the control room*.

Clenching his hands into fists, he spoke shakily.

"Sir, I'd be happy to help with whatever it is..."

Donnelly cut him off.

"Leave now before I decide that you're leaving for good."

Stevie paused for a second, decided that the chairman of the company very definitely qualified as authorised personnel, and legged it down the staircase as the interns scuttered along behind him, intern one reminding him of the regulations about unauthorised personnel as they went.

Before they'd descended one floor, Fraser was in the control booth, manipulating the computers and the many cameras at The Corporation's disposal. Fraser scrolled and erased and altered data and footage with elaborate flicks of his fingers, removing any trace of the private-feed footage that had been running since the teens entered the hospital. He checked the log: his name alone showed as the only board member to have accessed the private feed that night.

Taking a second to whisper a thank you to whoever, he performed a few more steps, removing his own personal access to the feed also. With that, all that remained was to get the boy and his friend off the hospital grounds before the power grid sprang back into life and the choppers brought the compound's staff back.

Praying that they'd have left by now, without running into Bracha, Fraser looped a finger in the air and tracked the kids to the main building.

They'd been searching the rooms nearby and were headed towards the fire exit, where a badly beaten Bracha was restrained to a radiator. Fraser permitted himself a wry smile. The smile vanished when he flipped his finger to engage the camera feed from the building's exterior.

Fraser swore loudly and crashed his fist onto the console when he saw Somna and fifty or so of his murderers at the hospital fences.

Fraser checked the time. The power would return in less than ten minutes. They didn't have time to deal with Bracha and find an escape that didn't put them straight into Somna's hands. They weren't even aware that time was a factor. So far as the teens were aware, the hospital was always in this empty state. He was certain that Somna would never enter the hospital grounds. That was the agreement he held with The Corporation. That left only one option. He reached for a secondary control console, wished for another Glenmorangie to steel himself, straightened his suit, made his hair a little more presentable and went to work.

Chapter 26

Alys

As they made their way back to Bracha, Alys glanced once more at the logo on the walls. Something itched her brain. She hadn't seen the logo before – she was certain of that – but the phrase 'UKBC'. It looked familiar. She shook it off and continued after Joey.

Reaching the fire exit where Bracha lay strapped and unconscious, Joey knelt next to the man and delivered a hard slap across his face.

He choked on some blood and drool as he came to. Spitting it onto the white tile he leered up at them.

"Nothing smart to say?" Joey asked.

Unable to move his broken jaw, Bracha elected to stay silent.

"No? Oh, well. Sorry about the teeth by the way, those were really something." Joey pointed at the floor where three of Bracha's top incisors lay broken and bloody.

This time he did growl at them. Joey gave a humourless laugh.

"What you do to people and you're vain about your teeth? Get a clue."

Joey retrieved the laptop Alys had found and showed it to Bracha.

"I want you to show me how to use this."

Bracha shook his head.

"Then you're not much use to us, are you?" Alys said, removing her third Sai from her belt. As she stepped towards Bracha, a loud mechanical clunk reverberated through the building. Both she and Joey jumped at the sound. Bracha began to laugh in a sort of strangled gurgle.

His eyes moved to the doors and Alys understood.

"Joey, the door."

He moved to push the exit open, finding that it wouldn't budge. Alys ran back along the corridor, trying the other doors they'd been in and out of during their search. All were locked shut.

The only door they hadn't tried was the one next to Bracha. The Main Feed Router room. Both were surprised to find that it swung open without resistance.

A voice came from inside the room.

"Please, do come in. I'm no threat to you, I give you my word. I want to help."

Alys moved through first, Joey backing in behind her. She scanned around the room. It was filled with black plastic boxes with red and green lights flickering away on them. The desks had keyboards, but no screens. The logo was emblazoned across the wall over the desks. Aside from electrical equipment the room was empty.

"There's no one here, Joey."

Joey turned and looked over the same equipment she'd just surveyed. He saw nothing that he recognised.

"I don't want you to be frightened."

The voice startled them. Both spun at once in the direction it came from – a little black box with a round opening.

"I'm going to turn on a…" The voice seemed to be searching for a word they'd understand. "I'm going to turn on a monitor. Do you know what that is?"

Alys answered. "Like a television?"

"Yes, like a television," he confirmed. "So that you can see me. Is that okay?"

Alys looked at Joey who shrugged.

"Yes. Okay." She told the voice.

Over one of the desks a bright light, shaped like a sphere, blinked into view. It spread out into the three dimensional form of a man's head and shoulders. They could still see through it. It wasn't solid, but made of light. Joey gasped.

Alys moved closer to look at the man. The man had greying hair cut neatly, more neatly than they'd ever seen a person's hair. His skin was unblemished, with no sores or old scars. Clean. He was dressed in a suit. His clothes looked as immaculate, as he did to Alys' eyes.

When he spoke, the image moved with his voice. It was like a ghost of a person's head sitting on a desk talking away, like it was the most normal thing in the world.

"What the hell is going on?" Alys demanded, suddenly angry.

The man looked sad for a second before snapping back.

"I'm sorry, but we just don't have time for explanations right now. Some very bad people are waiting outside for the man you have tied up. I'm going to open the fire exit. I want you to cut him free and let him out. He's in no shape to fight you again, and those people are no friends of his, I assure you."

Alys laughed at the man's image.

"You can't be serious? That monster?"

"I'm perfectly serious, Alys. Look here."

To the man's left a second image appeared, showing the outside of the building they were in. The fences still stood but on the other side of them a large group of men gathered.

Joey moved closer and peered at the faces of the men outside. Seeing a man kneeling beside a bound Zom on a flotilla, Joey cried out involuntarily.

"Somna."

Alys watched the man on the first screen as he stared at Joey's face. He looked sad and excited, and something else. An emotion that she couldn't place as he looked at her best friend.

"Joseph," the man said.

Turning to look at him directly for the first time, Joey glared at his image.

"Why have you locked us in here? Why lead us into this room? To gloat?"

The image of the man frowned.

"I want to help you get out of here safely."

Joey sprung away from him.

"We'll manage. Unlock the doors."

Alys watched the exchange, flicking her eyes from Joey's face to the man's. Something bothered her, but she couldn't place what it was.

"Those men... Somna's men, will do things to you that you cannot imagine, Joseph."

Alys felt Joey prickle at the man's repeated use of his given name. She stayed silent and allowed him to continue.

"Aside from them, the people who work in this building will return very soon. In six minutes' time every camera, every piece of electrical equipment in this compound will spring back into life. You will be seen by a huge number of eyes. The people who see you here, in this place, will have you killed for seeing it. Just for being here. If you listen to me, I have a route that you can leave by and they'll never know that you've been here; that you've seen this." He indicated the room around them.

Joey looked into the man's eyes.

"Why? Why are these people here inside the fences, with this technology? Are they security? In case survivors or the infected get near the fence?"

The man looked away from Joey's face for the first time since he'd come into shot and glanced at Alys apologetically before turning back to Joey.

"No... Nothing so noble. Look, Joseph, we have two minutes until there's nothing I can do for you. I don't have time for explanations. Go and cut Bracha free then get down there."

The man pointed to Alys' right where a panel had slid back in the floor, revealing a set of stairs leading under the building.

Joey was frozen in place, glaring at the man's image.

"Open the fire exit," Alys told him.

She stepped out into the hall, cut Bracha free and pushed him through the now-open door. A man with short, greying-black hair, saw her in the doorway as she threw Bracha to the asphalt. She slammed the door closed again and re-entered the feed room.

"Joey, come on." Alys put a hand on his shoulder.

He shrugged it off, continuing to glare at the man's hologram.

"Not until he tells me why. What are these people doing here? Why would they kill us for being here? Shouldn't they be helping us? We're not infected."

The man in the hologram image sighed and flicked at the air with a finger.

A screen to their right flickered into life and footage began to flip past.

Images of their lives. Images of them as kids. Of Jock being killed. Of Alys kissing someone Joey had never seen. Of a madman with a panda in his living room. Images of The Ringed eating survivors they didn't know. Of Jock as a younger man, fighting a herd of Ringed. Images of The Brotherhood in Communion, catatonic, praising The Children of Elisha.

It was obscene.

A voice boomed over the footage.

"Twenty-four hours a day, seven days a week, do not miss the next thrilling highlights episode this Thursday on UKBC."

A graphic covered an image of a Zom eating a child's intestines:

dEaDINBURGH

Exclusive to
UKBC

Alys and Joey stood stunned into silence, tears burning tracks along their cheeks. Joey fell to his knees.

"You watch us?" Alys voice was weak, distant. "We're trapped in here with monsters, fighting for survival, dying, and that's entertainment to you people?"

The man looked away.

"There's no time. They *will* kill you. Please. Go. The tunnel leads out to the woods to the back of the cycle path. We use it to bring new people in. There are no cameras, but there are speakers. I'll be able to guide you."

Joey rose to his feet.

"New people? Into this city?" The sclera of Joey's eyes was more red than white, his face a perfect mask of disbelief and betrayal. "That's why the fresh ones keep appearing," he said flatly to no one in particular.

"Judge later. You have twenty seconds before this is over for you. I'll ask you one question. Do you want to live?"

He nodded at the open hatch.

Alys pulled at Joey, who came along willingly now. As the hatch closed over their heads, Alys put all of her malice and hatred into a hard stare aimed at the man.

"One day, we'll find you."

The panel slid over as every instrument and panel sprang to life and the live feeds flickered back to life.

"I know." Fraser's holo-image muttered before flickering off.

Interlude

Fraser Donnelly

As the light for the holo-cam blinked off, Fraser sank back into his over-sized chair and let out a long sigh of relief. The instant the kids had closed the hatch behind them, the compound's electricity and security sprang back into life. *Too close.*

Swinging his seat a little to the lift, he watched Bracha make his way towards the tunnel he'd dug under the fence the night before. Bracha slipped under the gap the very instant that security had come back on line.

 Somna and his men had followed him along the fence-line towards the gap and had closed in on him as he rose to his feet on the other side of the fence.

Only ten yards stood between Somna's right-hand man, James Kelly, and Bracha. The rest of The Exalted were a hundred metres away. It appeared that Somna would finally have his ex-lieutenant back. Fraser cocked an eyebrow and smiled bitterly as he saw Bracha's probable fate in his mind's eye.

Flicking the image away Fraser watched the seconds tick past on the desk clock, timing the teens' journey along the tunnel towards the exit into the woods. After three minutes had passed, he activated the intercom to the tunnel's system.

"Alys? Joseph? Have you made it to the hatch yet?"

Fraser chewed at the inside of his cheek as he waited for a reply, worrying that they'd turned back, which was unlikely as the alarms would have gone off by now. Equally as worrying was the notion that they may have exited the tunnel already. Despite them having fought through a seemingly insurmountable number of Zombies at the same part of the woods the previous evening, the dead's numbers had tripled in the area since they'd last been there, drawn by the chance of a meal and the noise. Without him to guide them Alys and Joseph had zero chance of surviving in the woods, despite their extraordinary skills.

He tried again.

"Alys? Joseph?"

A voice cut sharply over his, crackling through the speaker.

"Can you stop calling me that? Call me Joey." He was trying to contain his anger, but it was a heat through the intercom.

"Okay, Joey." Realising that he hadn't given them a good reason to trust what he was about to tell them to do, he gave them the only thing he had to offer. His name.

"I'm Fraser."

"What do you want from us, Fraser?" Alys put a good dose of spite into his name as she pronounced it.

Fraser cleared his throat before speaking, burying the emotions swirling in him.

"I want you to survive." It was the simplest truth.

"For your viewers?" Joey asked scornfully.

Fraser lifted his chin, cricking his neck to the left to release some of the tension there.

"No, Joey. Not for them."

Their voices vanished for a few moments. Long enough to make Fraser believe that they'd left the safety of the tunnel. His finger hovered in mid-air, desperate to activate communication once more. His mind told it, *give them time*.

Finally the silence broke.

"Tell us what we need to know… then leave us alone." It was Alys.

Chapter 27

Joey

IN THE BLACKNESS OF THE TUNNEL, Joey finally felt in control again. He could concentrate fully and begin to try to absorb the revelations they'd been given. *Now isn't the time.* Joey snapped himself back to the moment, deciding that he could deal with the horror of their situation and his rising anger another time.

He held Alys' hand in the darkness to reassure her that he could see and to make himself feel less alone. Whilst the absence of light underground made him feel safe it also reminded him of how isolated he'd been in his former life. Or thought he'd been.

Joey listened as the man who called himself Fraser continued to give instructions through the little speaker bolted onto the tunnel wall.

"There are several hundred of the infected just through that hatch."

Joey glanced up to the top of a concrete staircase at the metal trapdoor, wondering if Fraser was stupid or just ignorant, that he thought he needed to tell Alys and himself that outside was teeming with the dead. Their groans, as familiar to them as their own voices, drifted down to the tunnel. Joey had never heard so many in one place and gritted his teeth in response.

He's brought us here to die.

Fraser continued.

"If you step outside you'll die."

He was beginning to irritate Joey.

"You expect us to sit here, then... *Fraser?*"

Joey waited a moment. The man on the other end of the conversation was clearly taking a minute to compose himself.

Because he was lying?

"No." For the first time, Fraser sounded unsure of himself. Strangely it made Joey trust him a fraction more than before.

"I want you to step outside and simply walk through them."

Both Alys and he laughed loudly at the same time.

"C'mon, Joey. Let's get back up to the hospital corridors."

"No!" Fraser blurted. Both teens halted in response to his cry. It was the most genuine-sounding word he'd spoken yet. "I promise that they'll kill you if you go that way."

Joey pushed at his intercom button.

"And The Ringed will do what? Throw us a party?"

"No, Joey. They'll ignore you completely. If you do what I tell you to."

He couldn't make out the expression on Alys' face in the darkness, but expected that she wore the same mocking expression he did.

He pushed the intercom again.

"Oh, why didn't you say? Okey dokey. We'll just pop up there now, will we?"

Fraser didn't miss a beat, his voice as steady, as calm as ever.

"You've seen them do it before, is it really so hard to believe me?"

A series of mental images flashed through Joey's mind. He thought about the oldest Zoms found on

The Royal Mile. Those Zoms never attacked The Brothers, no matter how close they were. They simply fed on whatever The Brotherhood offered and wandered away when they were finished. Father Grayson taught them that it was because The Brothers were God's shepherds. He asserted the dead knew that The Brothers were holy, that they existed to attend them.

Jock had told him many times of how often he'd cleared fresher Zoms from the fences of The Brotherhood at Grayson's command. Why was he worried about some Zoms and not others if The Brotherhood were God's shepherds?

"Go on," Joey said flatly.

Fraser's voice crackled through the darkness.

"I'm counting on you having some Carrionite in that bag of yours, Joey."

He'd been about to ask how Fraser knew about The Brotherhood's sacred powder, and then he remembered. *You watched it, you watched us, on TV... for entertainment. Every private moment.*

A surge of hatred coursed through him. He swallowed it back, giving a one word answer.

"Yes."

Joey hated that this man knew details of his life, maybe every detail. He felt violated. That Fraser knew he had Carrionite in his bag infuriated him. Joey hadn't even shared that knowledge with Alys. He didn't really know why he'd kept the Carrionite, other than as a reminder of his former home. He'd never taken Communion, never inhaled the powder or experienced its effects. The uninitiated Brothers were anointed with a simple cross marked in Carrionite on the forehead.

Joey couldn't hide his anger this time and growled into the intercom.

"Does that make you happy? Does it entertain you that you know these things, Fraser?"

"No it doesn't, but it does mean that you'll survive today."

Joey stabbed at the button with his index finger again.

"If you're trying to help, get on with it."

A beat of silence filled the tunnel before Fraser spoke again.

"Wet your faces, necks and the back of your hands. Do the same on any other exposed part of your body. We don't understand quite how the mechanism works, but the dead use a combination of sight, sound and smell to target… prey."

Fraser coughed before continuing.

"Their sense of smell is a mystery. The delicate membranes and sensory neurones are gone, but somehow their intellect, what remains of it, can still receive and process information from these senses. The sense of smell is actually quite developed..."

"Get on with it," Joey interrupted.

"Sorry. Okay, once you've wet those areas scatter as much Carrionite as you can over the wet areas and rub it in, forming a paste."

The teens had already wet themselves using puddles of stagnant water from the tunnel floor. Joey raked around in his satchel as Alys waited, eventually pulling out a grapefruit-sized leather pouch, tied at the top with a leather string.

Opening the pouch he told Alys, "Don't breathe any of this stuff in, or you'll lose a day."

He could feel her confusion, but pulled her close and began spreading it onto the wet areas of her skin until a fine coat formed over her.

The film of Carrionite that covered her reminded Joey of a time he'd contracted chicken pox and Father Grayson had bathed him in oats from The Gardens. A fine crust had formed on his skin then, and reduced the need to claw at the open sores that the virus had brought.

When he'd finished Alys repeated the process with him.

"What the hell is this stuff, Joey?"

He promised to tell her later.

"We're done," Alys informed the man through the intercom.

He sighed in relief.

"The ingredients in the Carrionite powder are formed from parts of the dead themselves. As well as the sensory effect it has on The Brotherhood during Communion, it also has a very powerful effect on the senses of the dead. Simply walk through them. The Carrionite will tell their senses that you're one of them."

"That's how The Brotherhood can walk amongst them? Worship them as they do?" Joey asked. He avoided saying *we* when referring to The Brotherhood.

"Yes," Fraser replied. "But you have to move slowly. Remember that they have other senses also. If you move with too much purpose or at a greater speed than they do, they'll notice you."

Alys brought herself close to him.

"Do you think this will work?"

Joey shook his head, forgetting for a moment that despite their closeness, she couldn't see him.

"It might. The Brotherhood were never attacked by the dead within their fences."

Joey jabbed at the intercom again.

"Does it work on the fresh ones?" Jock's tales of clearing the newly-dead from The Brotherhood's borders nagged at him.

"No," Fraser admitted. "The tissue still alive in them is fresh enough that their senses are much more acute. The eyesight in particular. You'll have to move slowly and hope that the fresher ones have mostly left the area. They're usually the first to realise that a food source is gone and wander off to look elsewhere."

"Don't you have cameras there?" Alys asked, her tone acid.

"We do, but I can't access them at the moment. The same people who would have detected you at the hospital had you been there when the power activated would notice me tapping the feed from here."

"So you're in as much danger as we are, are you, Fraser?" Joey's voice was filled with sarcasm.

"No, I'm not," Fraser said. "But I've done all that I can. If I'm to help you again, I can't be found by The Corporation at this time. Now, go. Time's running out for me too."

Alys climbed the first few stairs and lifted the trapdoor an inch, wincing as a flood of morning light shone through the gap. Joey saw that she had her Sai drawn. Before following along behind her, Joey pressed the intercom one last time.

"Thanks… I suppose."

He turned, drew his blades and emerged from the trapdoor side by side with Alys Shephard.

Standing in a small gap in an ocean of the dead, Joey peered through scrunched up eyes, confirming that Alys was there beside him. The weak winter sun was low in the sky and burned into his retina like a supernova. He cupped his hands over his eyes and gradually opened them, allowing small amounts of light, slowly increasing, into his eyes.

When they were fully open and the pain in his eyes had dulled, he scanned around. Alys was still beside him. Sai drawn but hanging low at her sides, she stood looking out over the hundreds of decomposed faces gathered around them. Former doctors, paramedics, and dozens of other types moved like a wave around them but not one of those faces turned towards the pair.

No eyes darted to their faces, no hands clawed at them, no teeth closed on their flesh or snapped at them from afar.

Joey felt invisible. Feeling his confidence grow, he stifled a laugh of joy before it escaped and took several steps out into the undead sea. He didn't try to resist but moved with the motion of the dead around them and gestured for Alys, whose eyes were wide with joy, to join him.

Allowing the movement of the dead to carry them along like a current towards the field where few roamed, Joey relaxed and surrendered to the rhythm. He felt peaceful. The surrender was exactly what he needed. In a mass of bodies, in various states of decomposition and with putrid smells all around, he felt truly alive for the first time since Jock had died. The anger that had been growing inside him since Jock had been killed had threatened to become a furnace of rage when he'd discovered the truth about their city. This moment, the passiveness of it, dampened that anger to an ember.

Something hard snagged and pulled at the leg of his trousers as he was carried along. Reaching down he found one of his arrows protruding from the head of a Zom. He yanked it out and began scoping around for others. The path the dead took towards the open field where they scattered carried him within reach of thirty of his arrows by the time he'd reached it.

Feeling a disappointment he hadn't expected upon disengaging from the tangle of creatures, he took Alys' hand and pulled her close. *To hell with it.*

He pulled her firmly towards him, and held her tight, celebrating their survival. Joey expected a punch in return, but it was worth it.

She dropped her Sai and clenched his face between her hands, locking him in a very brief kiss.

"You bloody stink like a Zom," she laughed quietly and gave him the punch he'd been expecting. In all honesty, he'd have been disappointed not to have been hit by her. It was what she did.

Alys noticed something over his shoulder.

"There are a few fresh ones up over there."

She pointed them out.

"Let's go around," she suggested.

"Go where?" Joey asked. The weight of everything they'd been through and had discovered settling heavily upon him.

Alys shrugged like it was the most obvious thing in the world.

"Home."

Joey stood still, feeling the chill of the morning wind on his skin as Alys gathered her weapons and her belongings.

Home.

Joey didn't really have a home anymore. The Royal Mile had been a prison, a lie. His time with Jock had been liberating and brought with it a parent at last, but had been far too brief.

The boy from The Brotherhood was long gone and Jock's apprentice had grown up. Where did this Joey belong? Who was he now? Someone whom eager viewers watched struggle to survive for their amusement? Maybe they really cared about him in their way.

How many others in Edinburgh were suffering for entertainment for the masses?

He pushed the thought of the cameras and a world outside of the quarantined city away. It was too big. The thought of the outside world and the callousness of the people there was too horrific a truth. *Later*, he told himself. *Deal with it later.*

Finally he decided that, whoever he was or whoever he was becoming, he was certain of two things about this young man who stood in a field, carried there by the dead.

He would forever cherish the memory of his foster-father, Jock, and use the skills he'd taught him, and he was blessed to have Alys Shephard for his best friend.

Throwing his rucksack over his shoulder, Joseph MacLeod followed his only friend through the long, crisply-frosted grass… Home.

Epilogue 1

James Kelly

Bracha emerged from under the fence-line, snaking quickly through the pit he'd dug under it to gain entry the day before. James strolled towards him, unhurried and came to a stop a few feet away from the spot where Bracha had already risen to his feet.

James wasted a second he couldn't afford with a quick appraisal of Bracha's condition. The teenagers had clearly done a job on him. Moving his eyes over the broken-looking man, James caught a broken nose and jaw, two badly damaged hands hanging useless and, from the ragged way he breathed, they'd done a number on his ribcage as well. A lopsided grin spread. He wasted another second with a glib comment.

"Kids, eh?"

Unsurprisingly, Bracha didn't laugh. He just stood there, body a ruin, eyes darting between checking over James' shoulder and glaring at his former friend.

James sighed and nodded over his shoulder.

"They're right behind me. Tell me the girl's name and I'll give you a head start. For old times' sake."

James had no intention of letting Somna get his hands on Bracha. Too many secrets would be learned. He wished he had it in him just to kill the beast who wore his best friend's face.

Bracha's eyes lit up, the embers of hope.

Through gritted teeth and clenched jaw he rasped, "Alish."

"Make it look good," James said, a half of a second before Bracha knocked him to the grass with a front kick that was more vicious than required.

As Jimmy Kelly watched Bracha limp into the woods, his brain treated him to a wee slideshow of images from his life as he blacked out. Random moments flickered and changed.

The Gardens. Breaking the soil there, growing corn, oats, peas. Himself and Cammy living a life there, a good life. A happy life.

Married life.

Images of their expulsion from The Gardens flew past in a flurry of madness and violence and irreparable deeds.

Images of Bracha, when he was still a good man. A prince among men. Literally.

He watched a scene of himself joining Bracha amongst The Exalted when every shred of decency in him screamed that it was wrong. Lying, always lying, walking the knife's edge with Somna. Keeping him away from the city with lies, lies, lies.

Cammy's death flashed past, the promise he made to him as he watched his friend turn from a good man into just another empty shell shambling through the city.

"Alys."

The name escaped James' lips as he passed over into unconsciousness. And then a final little reminder, his promise to keep.

Never let the madness in the south come to The Gardens, to Alys. Keep her safe.

He'd said the words and he'd meant them with all of his soul. He'd never let The Exalted know of the city communities. He'd do anything to keep them away, even become one of them. He'd inked his single raven under his eye for Cameron Shephard.

A single black tear to remind him why he was what he was and where he was. To protect Cameron Shephard's daughter.

Epilogue 2

Fraser Donnelly

Fraser sat by his intercom, absent-mindedly clearing the drives and all traces of his activities on the systems and replacing them with signs of an audit having been performed during his time in the control room. His heart raced with the adrenaline that had been consistently flooding his system over and over since the previous night's discovery of Joey and Alys' presence at the hospital compound. It had been an excruciating experience but, he had to admit, an incredibly exhilarating one.

Joey's voice suddenly broke through, snapping his attention back to the little speaker.

"Does it work on the fresh ones?" Joey's voice had become a little less aggressive. The boy was still pissed at him, but was obviously beginning to consider his plan.

He made a gesture and the link to Joey and Alys crackled back into life.

No," he said, reluctantly. "The tissue still alive in them is fresh enough that their senses are much more acute, the eyesight in particular. You'll have to move slowly and hope that the fresher ones have mostly left the area."

It was pathetic advice, but it was all he had to offer. If he were a religious man he might say a prayer but he'd abandoned the right to that particular privilege decades before.

"They're usually the first to realise that a food source is gone and wander off to look elsewhere."

"Don't you have cameras there?" Alys asked.

The accusation in her tone stung him. It had been a last resort to show them the footage being streamed from the abandoned city that they called home. Fraser had no idea what the fallout might be, particularly once they began discussing, on camera, the revelation that they were the subjects of history's cruellest *reality* programme. Its cruellest and its most successful, by a huge margin. dEaDINBURGH had been a hit for decades. A global hit.

"We do, but I can't access them at the moment. The same people who would have detected you at the hospital had you been there when the power activated would notice me tapping the feed from here."

"So you're in as much danger as we are, are you, Fraser?" Joey's voice mocked him over the miles and the reality that lay between them.

"No, I'm not," Fraser said. "But I've done all that I can. If I'm to help you again, I can't be found by The Corporation at this time. Now, go. Time's running out for me now."

Fraser listened to them open the trap-door above and then silence. It was time to get out of here, go downstairs and act the efficient boss. Toss around a few admonishments about their systems, and a few compliments too. All that would be left then was to get to his office and check on Joey and Alys.

dEaDINBURGH had been looping highlights footage in the time the show had been off-air. Now the standard twenty-four-hour coverage was back in place. He'd have little trouble discovering their fate.

He stood and pulled on his suit jacket. Smoothing the lapels down, Fraser adjusted the cuffs, sitting them at the appropriate length, peeking out from underneath his sleeves.

As he prepared to leave, hoping that the teenagers' presence had gone unnoticed by the infected, a voice crackled through the intercom.

It was Joey.

"Thanks… I suppose."

A wave of sadness, guilt, anger and grief passed through every cell in the organism named Fraser Donnelly, almost bringing him to his knees.

Composing himself he coughed the lump from his throat, flipped the light switch and replied to no one.

"You're welcome… son."

End of Book One

Bonus Content

Excerpt from dEaDINBURGH: Alliances (Din Eidyn Corpus 2)

Edinburgh, Scotland
2051

Jack

NOTICING LIGHT BREAKING through the gap in his curtains, Jack squinted at his Holo-Screen, blinking the fog from his eyes. Seven a.m.

He'd been playing the *dEaDINBURGH: Lair of The Ringed* video game since midnight, when the feed had been cut from the live show. He flicked his finger across the air in front of him, causing the UKBC screen to pop up. The countdown until the feed re-connected sat at 00:15. Just fifteen more minutes until they had the show back in full High-Def Holo-Image. Jack saved his progress and kicked at the desk in front of him, sending his ergonomic chair scooting backwards through the pile of empty energy drink cans and takeaway boxes littered across the carpet of his living room.

Scratching at his crotch with his right hand, he lifted his left arm and sniffed at his arm-pit, screwing his face up at the sourness. *Should have time for a shower if I get a move on.*

Jack stood with a groan in protest at the crack of his knees. It'd been a while since he'd had quite so long a session on the game. Scooping a handful of Cheesy-Puffs off the desk and into his mouth, he headed to the apartment's little shower cube.

As he sang from the shower, the dEaDINBURGH theme began blasting from the surround-sound speakers, eliciting a whoop of delight from him as he barrelled from the bathroom, not bothering to dry himself, body wobbling back into his still-warm chair.

Leaning forward he made a little gesture to enlarge the screen and scanned the info-bar along the bottom of the page to catch any updates. There were too many to read so Jack flicked a finger at the Holo-Screen, bringing up a highlights reel on a smaller screen within the main one. Whilst the main screen flickered into life, he jerked his eyes to the highlights feed, gleaning everything he could about what had happened to his favourite *Survivors* during the feed-loss.

Suzy Wheels, Danny McGhee and Jennifer Shephard, his main characters, were all more or less where they'd been when the feed had cut twelve hours earlier. Jack flicked at the screen a few more times, bringing up images of one of the less popular and least-covered *Survivors* he'd been following.

Joey MacLeod's face filled the frame. Jack liked this kid. He'd begun to get a little more airtime recently, mostly because he'd been in a few scraps with Zoms of late. Jack remembered him fondly from the episodes where he'd left The Brotherhood a few years back, with the old Padre. Those were amongst some of the most unexpected and emotional scenes he'd ever watched and he'd replayed them many times in his mind's eye, lying in bed.

Padre Jock had been a favourite of Jack's as a kid. As a Zom-Hunter and one of the most colourful characters on the show. He'd had a huge chunk of airtime over the years and had consistently been in the *Survivors'* top ten chart for over twenty years. When he'd been killed by Bracha, Jack had shed a few tears for the old man. For Jack's generation, who'd grown up watching him, Padre Jock was as intricately tied to the show as its theme tune.

Three years later, Jack still felt grief whenever he looked at one of the many images of Jock on mugs, posters, T-shirts and other merchandise around his home. Jack had a massive poster of Jock over his bed. It depicted a scene from the show with a young Jock, blades flashing, silencing five Zombies. It bore the legend: *Running rings around The Ringed.*

One of Jack's online friends had a tattoo on his cheek in the shape of the characteristic Ring o' Roses rash of The Ringed. Despite being into its third decade of transmission, dEaDINBURGH showed no signs of losing popularity, and if anything it had gained more viewers than ever. In part this was because of Jock's protégé Joey and his best friend, Alys Shephard. Quite simply she was the most skilled combatant the dead city had.

Many of Jock's fans had now latched onto the eighteen year old he'd trained out of the need for a connection to the familiarity of the Padre. Aside from that, they'd grown to know and love Joey during his time with Padre Jock. Many more had chosen Alys as their new prime *Survivor* because of her attachment to Joey and her own considerable talents. The pair were fast becoming the definitive *Survivors* of their generation.

The screen Jack scanned showed Joey and Alys, from behind, in a large open field. Joey had his bow over his back and was following along behind Jennifer's daughter. Their body language suggested they were tired and were both covered in grey dust. Jack watched as the cameras zoomed out, revealing a mass of Zoms spilling out into the field from a cycle path and a little clearing in a woodland. From the trail in the long grass, it was obvious that the teens had come from the Zom-infested area.

It was a beautiful shot, so much so that it moved Jack to click the little *thumbs-up* icon at the corner of the screen. He was only the hundredth to do so. It made him feel a part of something special that he was amongst the first to see the beauty in the photography.

Wondering how the teens had survived the massive congregation of Zoms and why the infected weren't pursuing them, he whirled the highlights footage over to the main screen and began searching through it, hoping that he hadn't missed something special. He looked at the view counter at the edge of the highlights screen.

One view.

A single viewer besides him.

Jack felt a thrill surge through him and clicked the *thumbs-up* icon, making himself the second person to have done so. He watched amazed as Joey and Alys moved like crowd-surfers along a mass of the dead. They seemed completely calm, so at ease as they slipped through and over a swarm of the Ringed. Jack had never seen anything like it.

Nobody had.

As the scene progressed, it was suddenly cut with footage from earlier in the day. The pair had battled hundreds of the dead in that same clearing, Joey with an injured foot in a tree firing arrows, and Alys a whirling, kicking and stabbing demon with her twin Sai. The images were astounding and contrasted so sharply with the serenity of the previous footage that Jack felt a prickle all over his skin.

He watched Joey and Alys' *Survivor* ratings rocket from around ten thousand straight to positions two and one, respectively. Realisation suddenly made him jerk in his seat. He motioned at the screen and watched as his viewer rating appeared. Last night he'd been somewhere close to the ten-million region. A respectable position for someone in Kent. The total viewing figures worldwide for dEaDINBURGH were at around four billion.

Due to his early support for Joey, and lifelong support of Jock, whom he'd voted for and thumbed-up hundreds of times, maybe thousands, in his lifetime, Jack's viewer rating would receive a boost. Factor in his support of Alys by proxy of being a Jennifer Shephard supporter, and combined with this morning's early acknowledgement of both the live-feed and the highlights package, and Jack's viewer rating should be at an all-time high, perhaps in the top one million.

Jack blinked in disbelief as he looked at the numbers.

His rating had been propelled into the Top 500, worldwide. Number 1 in Europe.

His Holo-Screen suddenly lit up with emails, messages and invitations regarding interviews, expert analysis and insights he might be happy to offer. He was being lined up for a series of appearances across some of the biggest shows on the network and a clutch of major blogs and newsfeeds. Hell, a news-crew were on their way to his apartment at that very moment.

Messages of congratulations from his network-family scrolled across his screen. In an instant he'd gone from being another nobody – an above-average fan who spent a little too much time watching the most-watched Holo-Programme on the planet and one of those guys who haunted the thousands of fan sites and pages looking for insights and extra-footage – to the hottest viewer-consultant in Europe.

Jack's eyes glazed as he considered the possibilities. He'd always known that he was someone special. Always felt that he was destined for something better than his current station in life. Something more important. His great-grandmother had been an exceptional woman, the first woman to become a true world leader. His own father, Mark, was a world-famous author. Sure, Dad had ridden the coat-tails of his grandmother too, but his books continued to sell well years since the old lady's death.

Jack conjured up an image of his father, Mark, with his arm around him, congratulating his son, expressing his pride. He watched his fiction-writing father and himself plan interviews and write opinion pieces together. He teared-up as an image of himself spoke to an audience of billions whilst his father stood at his side, beaming with admiration.

This was it. Finally.

Jack glanced down quickly at his mostly-naked wet body, edges of the towel barely meeting around and under his belly. He gave a curt, decisive nod, to himself. *Time to get sorted. The first thing I'll do is get that liposuction and skin removal. And my teeth. Get my teeth fixed. Pectoral implants. The UKBC will pay for everything, they always do for their correspondents.*

With the kudos and the money that'd be coming his way, it was time to get himself together.

Rising from his seat, he stopped for a second, lifted his right thigh a little and expelled a cloud of gas before heading to his wardrobe. Drying off, he pulled on a pair of clean sweatpants, figuring that he'd aim the Holo-Camera from the waist up. *Best to be comfortable.*

Jack then pulled on an old dEaDINBURGH T-shirt his dad had given him on his thirtieth birthday, with an image of Jock in full Plague-doctor outfit on the front. It felt a little tight, but also felt familiar.

Striding back through to take his seat, he flicked open the Comm for his first interview with an American news network, allowing himself to enjoy a moment of satisfaction at finding his rightful place.

Jack Thatcher smiled warmly and connected his call.

Interlude

This is how it feels to be Stephanie

I close my eye, the only one I have left. It leaks tears constantly, as though weeping at the loss of its twin. The empty socket itches, especially when I move the muscles. It's startling, the number of wee mannerisms, tics and idiosyncrasies we have in different parts of our bodies. Fidgeting fingers, flicking eyebrows, blinking patterns and tapping toes. They're just there. Unproductive and unnoticed, until the part that needs to scratch that habitual itch is gone.

My eyelids, with nothing beneath them to shield, still try blink in reflex. They narrow in bright light and widen in the dark.

I wear a patch.

The strap tugs at my hair and is causing friction burns at my cheek. I concentrate on those discomforts. I can't stop the subconscious habits of a lifetime and I can't prevent myself from feeling the attempted movement of the missing eye, but I sure as hell don't need to watch the muscles and lids around the gaping emptiness in action.

I feel alone and scared and vulnerable. My body shakes for no reason. I startle at sounds that have been regular, commonplace, my whole life. I've been training with Aunt Jen and I feel the limits of my soft body and bruised soul much more acutely under the regime she has chosen to torture me with. No… I chose the path.

I'm in control.

I detest myself for being so weak, so helpless at the hands of a monster. I'm beginning to feel hard muscle under the youthful fat. My archery strengthens as my arms do likewise. I hit eight moving targets out of ten. I can see an escape from the fear. A way to stop being the cowering, stupid little girl and become better. I won't ever be vulnerable again.

Chapter 1

Joey

Joey pulled the straps of his rucksack tighter, making his shoulders ache with the force. He hardly noticed. In his right hand he twirled a small rubbery object along his fingers as one might have done with a coin in times past. He walked and twirled and thought of his mother.

Dying, Jock had clung to the fraying fibres of life long enough to give him the flash drive he now fidgeted with and to relay the awful truth of the mother who died to save him as a new-born.

"Her name was Michelle. Michelle MacLeod. She wasn't from here, Joseph." Jock's last words replayed through his head as his gut heaved. *"The way she*

was dressed, the way she spoke, it was all wrong… Someone put her in here. From outside."

Joey felt the full impact of Jock's words at that moment in a way he never had before. Jock had died telling him of Michelle MacLeod, but instinctively Joey had compartmentalised the anger, the horror that his mother had been free, living outside the rotted city.

He'd focused all of the hurt and rage which had washed over him in the wake of Jock's death and his mentor's revelations of Michelle's appearance. Both barrels of that loss had blasted him in the heart and threatened to cripple him emotionally; threatened to rob him of his reason. He'd taken the strength of anger, of revenge, and made finding and killing Bracha the centre of his world for long enough to survive the storm of grief.

Now that he'd learned first-hand how cruel the people outside the fences were it brought a new and all-consuming surge of anger and sense of betrayal to him. He was trembling.

Joey leaned over and vomited into the moss-filled gutter. Glancing up, he noticed Alys still ahead, facing the other direction, running along. Wiping roughly at his mouth with the back of his sleeve, Joey walked onwards.

The haar was closing in. Hanging low it crept far into the city centre that evening. Joey had never considered whether the haar was a weather quirk unique to Edinburgh or if it swirled through and filled other cities. Why would he? The outside world was an abstract concept… until now.

Now, he couldn't stop thinking about the outside world and the monsters who lived there. The more he thought about the larger world, the angrier he became. The world outside had shifted cataclysmically from being inconsequential, an unnoticed constant, to being the only thing allowed space in his thoughts. He was filling up with hatred and he didn't know how to stop himself being consumed by it.

He watched the cold mist whirl above and along the streets of South Bridge as he trudged with heavy step and dark thoughts along after Alys. She was spinning and twirling along the roofs and bonnets of a continuous line of rusted cars along the main thoroughfare of the wide street. Normally he'd have somersaulted and twisted his way along the cars with his best friend, but not today.

Upon leaving the open meadow in Liberton, having swum a sea of the dead thanks to Fraser's advice. This man from the outside had communicated with them and saved their lives by imparting the knowledge that the Carrionite Joey carried from his time with The Brotherhood would render them both undetectable to the Ringed. The friends had spent the day stealthily travelling back towards the city.

Keen to avoid Somna's Exalted tribe, and any other prying eyes, they'd wound their way through Drum Wood, backtracking several times to lay false trails in the frost and earth, thus concealing their true route. The journey had taken hours longer than it should have, but the lost time was a price worth paying for safety.

As they'd travelled, the elation that Joey had felt on escaping the hospital and surviving the tide of The Ringed had faded quickly. As the full impact of Fraser's revelations hit him, his mind had begun to race with fear, anger and hate for the miserable bastards outside the city's fences who so casually and ruthlessly used the decaying world inside Edinburgh's fences as a source of entertainment.

He found himself examining every surface, each tree and dead lamppost, anywhere for signs of cameras or other devices. That people watched him at any and every given moment was threatening to immobilise him. Fearing he may vomit once again, Joey rested his behind on the bench-bar of a former bus stop.

He took a deep breath and let it loose in a long sigh, intended to banish the dark thoughts from him and clear the turbulence inside. He performed the ritual ten more times but felt no ebbing of the torrent of raw hate coursing through him. His heart began racing. He became aware that the world was swirling in an axis out of synch with the one he'd been attuned to for almost twenty years. He'd swear on his life that this was true.

A moment or two later, he opened his eyes to find Alys standing over him, one hand on his right cheek.

"Did you fall, Joey?" Unsure if she should be concerned or not, she looked like she wanted to smile. The notion that Joey, the free-runner, would slip and fall obviously tickled her.

Sweat beaded on his forehead and chilled his spine underneath the layers he wore to guard against the Edinburgh winter.

"No. I didn't fall," he said, rising to his feet. He felt the earth tilt again. Alys reached for his arm to steady him. He pushed her hand angrily away. "I'm fine, Alys."

Focusing on a broken padlock on the heavy, faded-red doors, Joey blinked several times, forcing his vision to clear and the ground to stay under him. Alys's jaw bunched and clenched in annoyance but she stayed quiet whilst he composed himself. Joey was exhausted. Physically he was fine, despite all the falling around. Mentally, he was drained. He was replaying in his mind's eye the footage Fraser had shown them. Every frame, crisp and clear. Each shot a bullet to his resilience. Each horrible discovery a blow, destroying his world. His head swam again.

"Let's camp here for the night. We can go to The Gardens tomorrow morning."

He looked around at Alys. She clearly wanted to push on, but shrugged.

"Aye. Ok."

After forcing the sturdy doors they did a sweep of the store and found only a single inhabitant. One of The Ringed who'd been silenced with a screwdriver to the temple. From the decomposition, he'd been long dead, or undead. Hardly any tissue remained, except for the head which had a long beard still in place and some long, curled hair at its crown.

Alys pulled a faded photo from behind the shop counter and handed it to Joey before resuming her sweep of the shop. Joey looked closely at the faces in the photograph to distract himself from another acidic ball of bile that was threatening to explode from his gullet. Three people stood, two men and a woman, arms around each other, grinning broadly into the camera. They were young and happy. They looked like nice kids. Working in a comic shop, selling stories of heroes and villains.

One of the men was thin with black curly hair and a long beard that didn't hide his youthful face and the warm humour in his tired-looking eyes. The girl also looked kind. Covered in tattoos, she was full-figured, beautiful and funny and very much in charge. She was in Joey's mind, at any rate. The other man had short hair and was clean-shaven. He held two fingers above the girl's head to represent ears and pulled a silly face. The three looked entirely carefree. The image brought the faintest tug of a smile to the corner of Joey's mouth which vanished with a glance at the bearded Ringed slumped in the corner.

Noticing a picture beneath the creature's leg he tugged at it.

As he pulled, a thick magazine in a plastic bag came free from under the rotted leg bone. Joey looked at the pictures on its cover. Colour and black and white, the images were of people in unfamiliar clothes holding guns and other weapons. A kid wore a funny-looking hat and a gun belt. One woman held a Japanese sword. Faces of The Ringed were printed there also.

Joey screwed his eyes closed tight, holding back the acid once more. After a second, he pulled the magazine from its protective covering and flipped through its pages.

People, in America, fighting The Ringed. He shook his head as though this movement would aid his comprehension of the story in his hands. *Is this a newspaper?* Jock had told him about these. *Is this an artist telling of the early days of the plague? Has it spread to other parts of the world?*

Puzzled, Joey mouthed the unfamiliar words as he slowly read through the story whilst Alys secured the perimeter. A man in a hospital. Waking to a world of the dead. A search for his family. The Ringed. Georgia, USA.

Joey flipped back to the cover to read the title: *The Walking Dead TPB, Volume 1.*

Thumbing forward another few pages, he noted the date and the disclaimer. One word and a number screamed out to him: *FICTION ... 2009.*

Joey threw the book at the wall and screamed.

"More entertainment!"

Alys came running.

"What the hell, Joe?" She held her hands out at her sides, palm up.

He pointed at the graphic novel which lay face-down on a pile of decomposed paper and wood.

"That."

Joey watched as Alys flipped through the book.

"This was written before Outbreak Day, Joey. It's just a story."

Dropping his head and his eyes down to hide his emotions, Joey said quietly, "I know. That's all we are to them."

He felt Alys come close and braced himself for her customary punch to the arm. Instead she brought her lips close to his ear and breathed into it.

"Not now. Let's talk later... Quietly.

She took a half-step back. Her thumb, shielded by her body, jabbed at the wall behind her. A very small camera, dusty and cracked, was perched in the corner. Neither trusted or even liked Fraser, but his words and actions had made it plain that they'd be in danger if it became known that they'd discovered that the outside world watched. Neither of them had any idea if the camera still functioned but they'd agreed on the journey not to discuss events at the hospital until they could be sure they wouldn't be observed or listened to.

Joey sighed. Turning away he busied himself with helping Alys secure the room. Working in silence, Alys barricaded the door to the basement, to save them having to search downstairs. Joey mechanically went through his routine of setting the wires and bells that would waken them should anyone, living or dead, stumble upon their camp. He could feel Alys watching him work and ignored her. She wanted to talk later, undercover in whispers. He didn't.

Retrieving from his bag a couple of apples they'd found in the woodland he threw one to Alys and sat on his sleeping bag to eat the other. After a few moments, Alys joined him. Sitting with crossed legs she crunched into her apple and appraised her best friend.

"Want to talk?" she asked between bites.

"No," Joey replied without looking up at her.

Alys spent a few more minutes crunching her apple to the core and staring at the top of his head as he ate.

"Yeah, well I do," she said finally, tossing her apple core into a dusty corner filled with mostly decomposed toy containers.

Joey looked into her eyes. His anger had begun to burn away and be replaced by grief. She could see the fragility of his mental state in his eyes. He allowed her to. She was his best friend and he needed to lean on her, absorb her strength, regardless of what he told himself.

Shaking his head, he made a gesture around the room.

"Undercover." He mouthed the words, a tear breaking loose from its duct as his lips moved.

Slipping under two sleeping bags, they hid themselves in a cocoon of nylon, warmth and grief. Hands cupped around ears and whispers, they sobbed and spoke and consoled and railed. They decided why and how to continue existing here in this place the outside world called *dEaDINBURGH*.

Finally, still hidden under layers of man-made warmth, holding each other, decisions and plans made, they slept.

----------End of excerpt--------

dEaDINBURGH: Alliances (Din Eidyn Corpus 2)

dEaDINBURGH: Origins (Din Eidyn Corpus 3)

dEaDINBURGH: Collected Edition

These titles are available on kindle and paperback from Amazon, US and UK as well as other formats at Paddy's Daddy Publishing.

Author's Note

When I set out to write this book, I'd sat at my desk with the intention of continuing with another novel that I was ten thousand words into. An image of a steaming hot baby, born fresh onto the cobbles of the Royal Mile in Edinburgh, surrounded by the clutching hands of the dead, shot through my mind and I started writing about him instead. Sometimes it's a worry, the shit that goes through my brain, often these random thoughts are dead-ends; but in this case, a novel emerged. A novel that I had amazing fun writing and, finally, one that my kids might be able to read whilst still young. Of all my people, I reckoned that my baby sister would like this book the most. So I wrote it for her.

This book was inspired by the fine works of Jonathan Maberry, Robert Kirkman and George A Romero.

Thank you for reading my book.

Please consider visiting Amazon UK, Amazon.US or Goodreads and leaving a review.

You May Also Enjoy:

Paul Carter is a Dead Man

by Ryan Bracha

"Bracha has established himself as one of the very best British authors, Indie or otherwise, with this wonderfully nasty, intelligent and exciting novel." - Mark Wilson, author of Head Boy and dEaDINBURGH

"True to form, Bracha projects scenery and characters in the back of your brain that play out like a brilliantly directed movie. Then he smacks you in the frontal lobes with his dark wit and wry humour. Paul Carter is legendary in a future Britain that makes Big Brother look like a bitch." - Craig Furchtenicht, author of Dimebag Bandits

In 2009 a bomb exploded, killing over 400 British citizens, including three generations of heir to the throne. Religious extremists took responsibility and the country went into meltdown. The British government was overthrown, and its troops withdrawn from overseas. The one-time empire closed its doors to the rest of the world. Law enforcement as it was no longer existed. The power was returned to the British people, and criminals were placed in online public courts for twenty four hours, to be judged.

The sentence for murder, death.

The sentence for anti-British behaviour, death.

The sentence for swearing, death.

In 2014 Paul Carter kills a man, and is now on the run. The thing is, Paul is smart. He's had enough of the new regime, and he's not the only one. He finds himself as an accidental revolutionary, and the voice of the disillusioned masses. He must learn to embrace the responsibility that has been thrust into his lap, and kick hard against a system which has failed everybody.

Paul Carter is a Dead Man is a horrifying glimpse into the future from the Amazon best-selling author of Strangers Are Just Friends You Haven't Killed Yet and is set to be the first book of the Dead Man trilogy.

Printed in Poland
by Amazon Fulfillment
Poland Sp. z o.o., Wrocław